UNCHARTED

❧ *A* GATES *Family Mystery* ❧

By Catherine Hapka

Based on characters created for the theatrical

motion picture, "National Treasure"

Screenplay by Jim Kouf and Cormac Wibberley & Marianne Wibberley

Story by Jim Kouf and Oren Aviv & Charles Segars

And characters created for the theatrical motion picture,

"National Treasure: Book of Secrets"

Screenplay by The Wibberleys

Story by Gregory Poirier and The Wibberleys & Ted Elliott & Terry Rossio

DISNEP PRESS

New York

Thank you to those who started this hunt:
Oren Aviv, Charles Segars, and Jim Kouf

And those who carry it on:
Christine Cadena, Jason Reed, Rich Thomas,
and Elizabeth Rudnick

UNCHARTED

❧ *A* GATES *Family Mystery* ❧

Printed in the United States of America

First Edition
1 3 5 7 9 10 8 6 4 2

Library of Congress Catalog Card Number: 2008924164
ISBN 978-1-4231-0875-7

Map Courtesy of the Library of Congress, Maps and Geography Division

This book is set in 13-point Centaur MT

Visit disneybooks.com

Spring 1803
Philadelphia

"Where is that twin of yours, Adam? I wish to ask her whether she has finished the embroidery she started yesterday evening."

Adam Benjamin Gates looked up from the Sheraton table in the front parlor of his uncle's city town house, where he had been flipping idly through the latest issue of *Port Folio* magazine. His mother's sister, Millicent, was peering at him, her thin, pinched face looking rather more sallow than usual beneath its purple silk bonnet trimmed in ribbon and marabout feathers. In the next room, the plunk and tinkle of a pianoforte interrupted the quiet of an otherwise sleepy afternoon.

"I don't know, Aunt Millicent," Adam replied. "Have you checked the kitchen? Perhaps she is there helping with the supper preparations."

1

"Ah, a clever thought, Adam. Thank you. I shall look straight away." Aunt Millicent gathered her skirts and hurried out of the parlor.

Adam's brother George, who was reading the newspaper in a comfortable chair near the fireplace, shook his head at his aunt's retreating back. Since turning eighteen that winter, he'd become rather bossy, even though he was only a year older than the twins. Ellie chafed a bit whenever George started acting like a mother hen worrying over her chicks. Adam, on the other hand, took very little in life seriously; he found his eldest brother's behavior humorous and had started referring to him with increasing regularity as "Grandpappy George."

"You know very well the kitchen is the very last place Ellie is likely to be," George said now, his broad, ruddy face disapproving.

Adam grinned and stood up. As he did so, he caught a glimpse of himself in the looking glass over the fireplace mantel. He paused just long enough to admire his own sandy brown hair. He'd recently had it cut in the modern style, short in back with a riot of longer waves falling forward over his high, pale forehead.

"I know," he told George. "I'd better warn her that Aunt Millicent is after her. Especially since I happen to know she got fed up with that embroidery last night and pitched it into the fire."

"Good luck finding her." George snorted. "Since our arrival in Philadelphia, Ellie has taken to keeping to herself more than is usual even for her. I don't think she is enjoying this extended stay with our relatives."

"True enough." Adam gave his brother a wave, then hurried out of the room, thinking that it was too bad that his twin sister was having so little fun on the visit. He was having a fine enough time of it himself, despite his grandmother and aunt's penchant for dull dinner parties and the minor irritations of bunking with his constantly squabbling young cousins. It was his first trip to the large and vibrant former capital city, and he found it much to his liking—considerably more exciting and cosmopolitan than sleepy old familiar Boston, the closest large town to his home in Concord, Massachusetts.

Then again, Ellie has never truly appreciated the charms of a bustling metropolis, he thought as he quickly checked all of Ellie's usual hiding spots within the house. *She has always been much more interested in nature and the outdoors, or in sketching her maps or reading about the latest scientific discoveries.*

At home, their parents allowed and even encouraged such things in their daughter, at least to a point. Lately, their mother, May, had started hinting that it might be wise for Ellie to develop some more traditional female interests and skills. In fact, Adam suspected that was one of the reasons for this visit. However, their father, John, had always seemed content to allow Ellie to contribute more in the stable yard than in the house, even though she was his only daughter. George said it was because of Aunt Alice. According to the older relatives, Ellie was Alice's spitting image in many ways, and Alice and John had always been close. Adam didn't know if that was truly the reason, but in any case, John Raleigh Gates accepted his daughter exactly as she was.

Unfortunately, John's Philadelphia in-laws did not share this tolerance. They considered none of Ellie's interests proper pursuits for a young lady, and Aunt Millicent in particular seemed determined to "fix" her during this visit.

If only Aunt Millie could see Ellie back home at the family livery stable covered in straw and manure after wrestling with a recalcitrant colt! That would be an amusing thing to see indeed, Adam thought, grinning at the image within his mind. *But never mind. At least we have only a few days to go before journeying for home once again. Ellie should be able to tolerate Aunt Millie and the others for that much longer.*

By now he found himself at the front door. Stepping outside, he glanced up and down the residential street. He was just in time to see a flash of moss green skirts disappearing around the corner.

"A-ha," he said aloud. "Now I have you. . . ."

It took him only a moment to catch up to the wearer of the green skirts, who was indeed his sister, Eleanor. With her was their eleven-year-old cousin Robert, a stout, fair-haired, dull-minded boy of no particular charm just like his mother, Aunt Millicent.

"It's no matter that Adam's caught us, is it, Ellie?" Robert demanded, his round, pink face petulant. "I'm still keeping the half eagle you paid me!"

"Better sleep with one eye open tonight, Robbie, or your gold coin may wander off," Adam teased, laughing as his young cousin howled in outrage. Turning to Ellie, he added,

"I'll come along on whatever adventure you're about if you don't mind. I'm weary of listening to cousin Charlotte practice the piano, and I wouldn't mind seeing a bit more of the city. There must be more riches to Philadelphia than the playhouse and the cotillion!"

"You're not thinking of those treasure hunters, the Brewster brothers, are you, Adam?" Ellie asked sharply. Her clear blue eyes, a mirror image of Adam's own, registered suspicion. "You know Father warned you against seeking them out."

Adam shrugged. "What if he did? He warned you against giving Aunt Millicent the vapors, and see how that's worked out, sister dear." He winked. "Besides, Father has no room to talk if even half the stories Uncle Duncan tells of their boyhood adventures are true. He was quite the treasure hunter himself back then, you know."

"That's as may be. But Father says the Brewsters are no good. They are only after treasure for selfish purposes."

Adam grinned and made a face. "Thank you for the advice, *George*."

"Are we going on, or returning home?" Robert spoke up, sounding impatient.

"We're going on," Ellie told him. "Show us the way, if you please, Robert. Thank you."

As they walked on through the cobbled city streets, half of Adam's attention was on the interesting sights they saw in passing—a fine-looking curricle pulled by a matched pair of flashy bays, several small boys chasing a group of hogs that had been rooting for refuse in the street, an old woman selling pepper pot on the corner. But the other half of his mind stayed with the topic of his father's interesting past. John Gates was kept busy these days running a successful livery and harness business with his sister's husband, Duncan Winslow, as well as being distracted by the demands of a wife and five children.

Even so, John maintained the keen interest in treasure hunting that had been passed down to him by his father, and Adam's grandfather, Thomas Gates, and the many generations before him. John had passed this interest on to George, who treated it as a hobby, sometimes rambling out into the woods near Concord in search of some minor booty. Adam himself found the whole idea of hunting for lost treasure appealing, and enjoyed stumping his younger brothers with codes and tricky riddles, though he rarely saw a need to join

George on his dull and often fruitless tramps through scratchy trees and muddy fields in hopes of finding a few coins or a bit of lost metal.

No, if I were to go on a treasure hunt, it would have to be for something worth the trouble, he thought now, glancing around the genteel neighborhood of distinguished-looking private homes through which they were passing. *Something at the very least like those vital munitions that Father and his friends uncovered when they were my age. Or better yet, one of the fabulous treasures of wealth beyond imagining that Grandfather sometimes talks about. . . .*

"Do you believe in the Lost City of Gold, Robert?" he asked as they walked.

His cousin glanced over, pulling a face. "'Course not," he said. "Nor that Treasure of the Ancients or whatever you may have it that you Gates cousins are always on about neither. Father says those rumors are all a lot of bunkum and balderdash put forth by rogues and believed only by simpletons." Then his face brightened. "Still, I know how I'd spend such a treasure if it *were* real. First, I'd buy up seven of the largest mansions in Philadelphia, and sleep in a different one for each night of the week. Then I'd get me as many apple dumplings and as much peanut brittle as I could eat. . . ."

"Are we going the right way, Robert?" Ellie interrupted. Of all the Gates siblings, only she seemed to lack any interest whatsoever in treasure. Like most of their neighbors back in Concord, she considered treasure hunting a greedy and foolish pursuit.

"Where *are* we heading?" Adam asked her.

"Robert says he knows where Captain Lewis might be today."

"Captain Lewis?"

She frowned. "Do you listen to nothing I say, Adam?" she exclaimed. "I'm talking of Meriwether Lewis, the officer President Jefferson has named to head his expedition to explore the uncharted land beyond the Mississippi River! The president has sent Captain Lewis here to Philadelphia to study all the sciences with the great minds of today, to help prepare him for the grand adventure."

"Oh. Of course." Now that she mentioned it, Adam did recall her saying such a thing several times during the journey down from Concord. Shooting a sly look in Robert's direction, Adam added, "I'm resorr, Lee-ell. I leetru should tenlis terbet."

"What's that?" Robert demanded sourly. "Stop it! You

know Mother and Grandmum have both told you not to tease me with your nonsense words."

Adam grinned. He and Ellie often used a playful code language of their own invention. They'd created it years ago simply by inverting the syllables in longer words—a habit which took some practice to master both in speaking and comprehending but one which, once learned, came nearly as naturally as ordinary speech. This secret language was useful when the two of them found the need to confound their other siblings or speak more privately in public places. During this visit, Adam had discovered that it also served to irritate his young cousins in a most satisfying manner.

"Ree-ver ree-sorr, Ertrob," he told the younger boy with an expression of great contrition.

"Oh, very well!" Robert spun on his heel, his face going red. "You can find your cussed Captain Lewis from here on your own, then. I'm off. And I'm still keeping the half eagle, so there!" Without awaiting a response, he dashed off and was soon lost to sight among the crowds.

"Well done, Adam." Ellie sighed and glanced at her twin. "Now what are we to do? You've chased off our guide and left us on our own in this unfamiliar city, with no idea where we're going. We'll be lucky to make it home in time for supper, let alone find Captain Lewis."

Adam shrugged. "No matter," he said easily. "We can treat it as a puzzle—a treasure hunt, as Father might do in our place. What do you say, tersis estdear?"

"What *can* I say, leesill therbro?" Despite her obvious attempt to maintain her dismayed expression, the corners of Ellie's mouth twitched with ill-disguised mirth. She never was able to remain annoyed with her twin for very long. "All right then. I suppose the family talent for treasure hunting might as well come in handy for once."

"Very well. Then the hunt begins. You said Lewis is studying with the great scientific minds of Philadelphia, yes?" Adam rubbed his hands together and glanced around. "Now, where might one find such illustrious and learned men, I wonder?"

They had left the residential neighborhood by now and were in a mixed area of homes and businesses. A tall man, well dressed in a dark brown coat and Hessian boots, was striding past at the moment.

"Begging your pardon, sir," Adam said, holding up a

hand to stop the man. "Might you be able to tell me where I could find Captain Meriwether Lewis?"

The man shook his head, looking slightly befuddled. "I know no such gentleman," he said brusquely.

The next few bypassers gave similar responses. "How odd," Ellie said after the third one, a woman carrying a basket of potatoes, had moved on. "People hardly seem to have heard of Captain Lewis. One would think his visit would be the talk of the city."

"Surely someone in Philadelphia must read the papers," Adam said, leaning against the brick wall of the nearest building. "Ah! I see a likely subject now." He pointed toward a young man coming their way. The man was tall and broad-shouldered with sleek, dark hair and an intelligent look about his sun-darkened face. Under his arm he held a few rolled-up parchments.

"But of course," the young man said as soon as Adam had posed his question. "I have just come from meeting with Captain Lewis myself."

"You have?" Ellie exclaimed, her face lighting up with excitement.

"Indeed." The young man bowed. "I am Private Hugh

McNeal. I have just this day volunteered and been accepted as part of Captain Lewis's voyage of discovery."

"My name is Adam Gates," Adam replied. "And this is my sister, Eleanor. We are visiting from Concord, Massachusetts."

McNeal politely shook Adam's hand. However, Adam noted with some amusement that the young man's gaze hardly left Ellie's face.

Ah, it seems Father is right when he tells Mother that it matters not whether Ellie is dressed in the latest fashions or has her hair done up in the proper way, he thought. *She still manages to attract admiring glances wherever she goes.*

"You are fortunate to be embarking on such an adventure, Mr. McNeal," Ellie told the young man with enthusiasm. "I am hoping to find Captain Lewis and volunteer for the journey myself."

"You?" McNeal looked politely skeptical. "I am afraid I do not know that anyone of the fairer sex would be accepted on a voyage filled with such dangers. But perhaps you shall be the first, Miss Gates." He bowed slightly and smiled at her. "If not, perhaps you would allow me to write to you about what I see on my journey? That way you can still feel a part of things from the safety and comfort of your own home."

"What a kind offer. Thank you." Ellie's words were calm and courteous. Adam suspected that he alone knew her well enough to detect the irritation in her eyes and the set of her jaw.

Hugh McNeal seemed not to notice any of that as he eagerly took down Ellie's address. "Now then," he said. "I can tell you that Captain Lewis is studying this day with the well-known physician, Dr. Benjamin Rush. Dr. Rush is a professor at the Institutes of Medicine at the University of Pennsylvania." He turned to Adam, giving him the directions, before returning his attention to Ellie. "I would show you the way myself, but I'm afraid I am already late for another appointment. Still, perhaps I can see you once again during your stay in Philadelphia?"

"Perhaps." Ellie smiled. "Thank you for your help, sir."

McNeal hurried off, and the twins set out the other way, following his directions. They rounded a corner onto Arch Street just in time to see a pair of men step out of a doorway halfway down the block. Ellie let out a gasp.

"That is Captain Lewis," she said, staring at the younger

of the men. "I would recognize him anywhere from the descriptions I have read."

Adam nodded, though he was distracted at that moment by a shout from an alley nearby. Taking a step closer, he peered in and saw a bedraggled woman clutching a young boy against her chest while three young men faced them in a threatening manner.

The woman had an ill, sallow look about her; her dress was dirty and patched. The boy was perhaps cousin Robert's age or a bit younger, though he otherwise bore little resemblance to the well-fed Robert, being as thin as a whip, with a shaggy head of dark hair, a narrow face with a pointy chin, and great dark eyes.

"Guttersnipe!" one of the men shouted. "You and your strumpet of a mother should not have shown your faces here."

"Please, sir!" the woman cried out with a sob. She paused to cough painfully into her sleeve before continuing. "We mean you no harm. . . ."

One of the other men spit a wad of chewing tobacco at the woman's feet, splashing the hem of her dress with greasy residue. "If that's true, what are you doing here instead of in Washington where you belong?"

"Adam?" Ellie said, coming up behind him. As soon as she took in what was happening, she pushed past her brother. "You there!" she cried, striding toward the men. "Do my eyes deceive me, or are you picking on these poor, defenseless people?"

The first man whirled around, his face registering surprise. He was four or five years older than Adam and a little taller. "And what business of it is of yours?" he demanded, his fists clenched at his sides.

"I must caution you, sir." Adam jumped forward in defense of his twin. "You would be better to speak to my sister with a bit more respect."

"Oh, really?" The man stalked forward, flanked by the other two. Judging by the similarity of their narrow, golden brown eyes and sunken cheekbones, Adam guessed all three of them to be related. "Well, and just who might you be, my lad?"

"I am Adam Gates of Concord," Adam replied with more bravado than he felt. "Who might you be, and what argument have you with this woman?"

"I am Stephen Brewster of Philadelphia, and these are my brothers Roger and Miles," the man retorted. "And I must ask again, what business is it of yours what discussion we have with this woman?"

Adam's eyes widened. "B-Brewster?" he stammered out in surprise. "Then you are the infamous Brewster brothers, the treasure hunters?" He could hardly believe the coincidence. In a city of more than forty thousand, what were the odds of encountering this trio?

Meanwhile, Ellie had pushed past the men, little concerned with their identity. "Are you all right?" she was asking the woman and child. The woman returned her smile cautiously, but the boy shrank back from her. "It's all right, little man," she told him kindly. "Here, would you like this?"

Adam couldn't see what she held out, though he saw the boy hesitate and then grab it. He was distracted by the Brewster brothers, all of whom had turned their curious golden brown eyes upon him. It was not a particularly comfortable feeling.

"So our fame has traveled as far as Concord, eh?" said Stephen, who appeared to be the eldest.

"Hey!" Miles, the youngest and slightest of the brothers, exclaimed. "Look at the little mice trying to creep away."

The woman and boy had been edging toward the far end of the alley, aided by Ellie. Now they froze, the woman's expression full of terror.

"Look, surely these two are nothing to you," Adam said, trying for a tone of easy jollity. "Why not let them go?"

Stephen Brewster glowered at him. "Do you care to force the matter, my friend?"

Meanwhile, Roger had stepped over to peer out the mouth of the alley. "Oi!" he called. "Lewis is on the move. He's getting into a carriage!"

That finally seemed to get the other brothers' attention. "Let's go," Stephen said. "We don't want to lose him." He paused just long enough to glare at the woman and boy over his shoulder. "But we'd better not see you two again, in this or any other city!" Glancing at Adam and Ellie, he added with a growl, "And that goes for the pair of you, as well."

The three of them rushed off. "Oh, dear," Ellie said, returning to her brother's side. "They were right. Captain Lewis is gone, and Dr. Rush with him." She slumped against the wall. "It seems I have missed my chance, at least for today."

"Oh, well. At least we've done our good deed for—hey,

where did those two go?" Adam interrupted himself, as a backward glance showed no sign of the woman and her young son. "And what did you give that boy, anyway?"

"Just a bit of candy. I brought it to help bribe Robert in case he became difficult." Ellie gathered her skirts and sighed. "Come on. We'd better find our way home before Uncle Edward sends out a search party."

Choux La
Bourhara L.
The Gate of Bend
Mandane I.
Missouri R.
Sioux I.
Plums I.
Anchelord
Arat I.
L it Mi
Chaguenne I.
Red T.
Blue I.
R. Plate or Shell
Panis L.
W. Fork
Saline R.
R. Plate Mts.
R. du Nord
S. Fork
S. Francisco
Carmelo R.
S. Laurent
S. Fé
R. Verardo
NEW
NAYA
Cornel
CALI

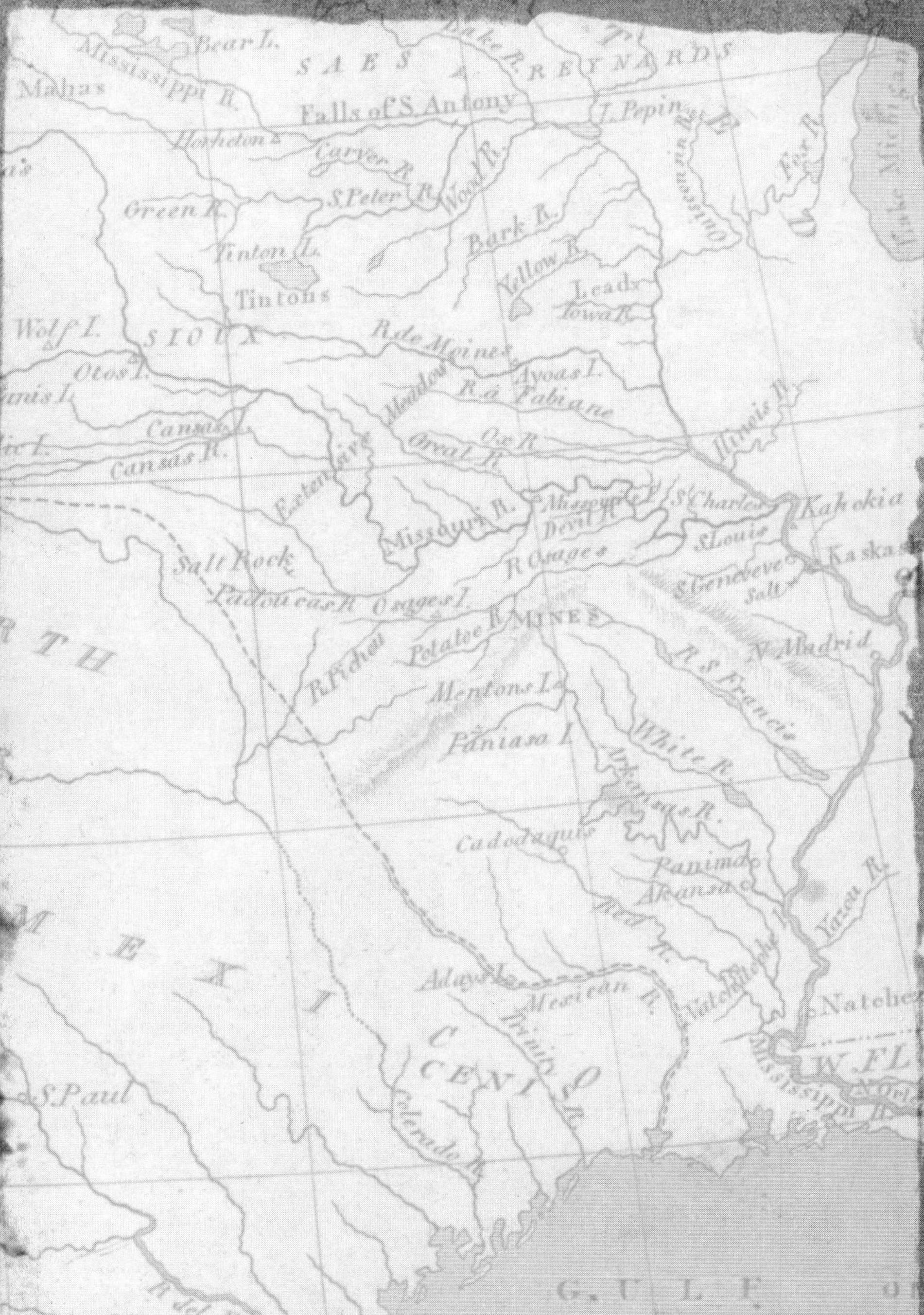

Bear L.
Mississippi R.
Mahas
SAES
REYNARDS
Falls of S. Antony
L. Pepin
Horheton
Carver R.
S. Peter R.
Wood R.
Green R.
Tinton L.
Tintons
Bark R.
Yellow R.
Leads
Iowa R.
Fox R.
Wolf I.
SIOUX
R. de Moines
Otos I.
Ayoas I.
R. a Fabiane
Meadow
Cansas
Cansas R.
Ox R.
Oreal R.
Illinois R.
Missouri R.
Devil R.
S. Charles
Kahokia
S. Louis
Salt Rock
R. Osages
S. Genevieve
Salt
Padoucas R.
Osages I.
Potatoe R.
MINES
N. Madrid
R. Pichet
Mentons L.
R. S. Francis
White R.
Paniasa L.
Arkansas R.
Cadodaquis
Panima
Akansa
Red R.
Yazou R.
Adayes
Mexican R.
Trinity R.
Mississippi R.
M E X I
C E N I
S. Paul
Colorado R.
R. del Nord
G U L F

One

"Adam! George! Dinner!" a cry rang out.

Adam looked up from latching a stall door behind a lazy chestnut mare. "Coming!" he shouted back. Then he looked around for his brother, spotting him coming out of the harness room at the end of the stable aisle.

"Did you check on the roan's hoof?" George asked.

"I checked it this morning. I'm quite sure it's still attached to his leg." Adam grinned. "Now come on, or I'll eat your share of Mother's chicken pie!"

He raced out of the stable, ignoring his older brother's grumbling. George was always ready to squeeze in one more chore before a meal, but Adam had been working hard all day and was hungry. He figured the horses could keep themselves for the next hour or so.

The sun was setting, the coming of night finally offering some relief from the heat of the July day in Concord. But inside the rambling farmhouse at the north end of the stable yard, the kitchen was steamy and warm thanks to the cooking fire in the stone-lined hearth. Ellie was setting the table with the help of one of the younger boys. Adam's mother, May, a pleasant-looking woman with a kind, intelligent, heart-shaped face, was leaning over an iron pot stirring something within. She straightened up when Adam entered.

"Any sign of your father yet?" she asked.

"I'm here, I'm here!" a voice called out before Adam could answer. John Gates hurried into the room, his shock of dark hair lank with sweat but a rather excited expression in his bright blue eyes.

At the same time, Adam's grandfather, Thomas, hobbled in from the sitting room with his cane supporting one thin arm and his youngest grandson the other. "Any news from town?" he asked John in his weak, quavering voice.

"Indeed!" John tossed his hat onto a hook near the door. "Everyone is talking of it. It has just been announced— President Jefferson has purchased the territory of Louisiana from Napoleon!"

Ellie looked up from her task. "Oh, my! But what does that mean for Captain Lewis's planned exploration?"

Adam shot her a look. She had spoken only occasionally

of the expedition since their return from Philadelphia some months earlier, but he suspected she thought of it much more often than that. He knew she was disappointed never to have had the chance to meet Captain Lewis.

At least Ellie's handsome and ardent friend Mr. McNeal has been true to his word so far about writing to her of his adventures, he thought with a flash of amusement. *The voyage of discovery has yet to begin, and she has already received nearly a dozen letters from him, and sent several in return.*

By now both John and Thomas had taken seats at the family's modest old sawbuck dining table. "It means Mr. Lewis will no longer be embarking upon a dangerous spying mission through foreign territory," John told his daughter as his wife began ladling out the evening meal. "Instead, it becomes an exploration of land mostly now owned by the United States."

"The Federalists be blasted!" Thomas put in with a cackle. "I suppose this means that dad-blamed Napoleon needed more money for his military adventures in Europe and the islands."

"Now, now, Thomas," May said soothingly. "No talk of politics at table, please."

"But this news goes far beyond politics, my dear," John said. "The purchase of the Louisiana Territory from France greatly increases the size of this country's holdings. As the esteemed Mr. Livingston is said to have put it, this shall allow our young nation to begin to rank among the first powers in the world."

Thomas spooned up some broth, but paused with it halfway to his mouth, staring into space. "And this Lewis fellow will have the opportunity to explore all of it and then some," he said. "If only I were younger, I would be rushing to sign up to go along with him."

"You and me both, Father," John said with a chuckle. "What an adventure that would be, eh?"

Thomas slid his watery old eyes in the direction of Adam, already seated, and George, who had just come in. "Ah, but there are two strapping young men here who are the perfect age for such an adventure," he said with a wink.

"That's enough, Thomas." May's voice was sharper than usual. "There are adventures aplenty right here in Concord for this family."

Ellie hardly seemed to have heard her mother. "Is there

any further word on when the great exploration will begin?" she asked her father.

John shrugged. "Not that I have heard. I believe they are still involved in making preparations."

"Speaking of the expedition, I heard an interesting rumor recently," Thomas spoke up again. He paused as a cough wracked his body. "A secret reason for President Jefferson to send Lewis in particular into the west. And this latest news makes it all the easier to believe."

"What is the reason, Grandfather?" Adam asked, recognizing the gleam in the old man's eye, which usually meant they were in for an interesting tale—if not always a credible one.

Thomas laid one finger beside his nose and smiled. "I hear the president might be sending Lewis and his party to recover the Treasure of the Ancients!"

"Oh, Father," John scoffed with a chuckle.

But Adam's heart started beating faster. The Treasure of the Ancients! He'd grown up on tales of that mystical collection of riches. It was said to date from the time of the Pharaohs or earlier, a treasure that had been fought over for centuries, growing larger throughout time to unimaginable levels of wealth.

"Think about it," Thomas went on. "Why else would the president go against his own stated adherence to the Constitution? Why else spend so much of the national treasury on five hundred million acres filled only with trees, wild creatures, and hostile native tribesmen?"

Adam considered the question. According to the family tales, it was rumored that the treasure had eventually made its way to the New World. The tales also claimed that knowledge of its current hiding place was known by only a small number of the great men of the day through their membership in the Freemasons, a brotherhood passed down from the time of the Knights Templar. Nobody seemed to know exactly which men might hold this secret, but it was commonly known that many of President Jefferson's closest friends and advisors were Freemasons, even if he himself was not.

What if it's true? Adam wondered. *What if the treasure really is the reason behind this expedition? It certainly makes a better excuse for trekking off through the untamed wilderness than the others I've heard named. . . . Who cares about the control of ports, or a water route to the far coast, or competing with England and Spain, or even scientific research? Not in comparison with a search for riches beyond all imagining. . . .*

✳ ✳ ✳

"Adam! Come here a moment, my boy."

Adam paused on his way past the sitting room. Glancing inside, he saw his grandfather huddled alone before the dying fire. Dinner had ended some time ago, and Adam had just come in from one last check of the horses.

"What is it, Grandfather?" he asked, stepping toward him.

When he got closer, he saw by the weak glow of the fire that Thomas was staring down at something in his hands— a round, battered-looking object about the size of a harness buckle. Adam immediately recognized it as the wooden medallion that had been passed down in their family for too many generations to count.

Uh-oh, Adam thought, a half-smile on his face. *Everyone knows not to get Grandfather started on that old thing. . . .*

To be fair, he didn't really mind listening to the story over and over again, not even when the old man started to ramble. Adam liked seeing the sparkle in the old man's eyes whenever he spoke of the medallion.

But there was no sparkle now when Thomas peered at his grandson in the dim light. "Adam, my boy," he croaked out, his voice hoarser than usual. "You know the story of this medallion, do you not?"

"Of course, Grandfather." Adam perched on a stool near the old man's chair. "You have told us that it comes from the first Gates to settle in the New World."

"That's right. My grandfather's great-grandfather, Samuel Thomas Gates." Thomas turned the wooden medallion over in his gnarled hands. "He received it from an old native woman, who received it from a man Samuel believed to be one of the missing settlers from the lost colony of Roanoke. He also believed the medallion was the key to a great treasure."

"And generations of Gates men have tried to crack its code since that day," Adam recited, knowing the story by heart. "None have yet succeeded, and so the mystery lives on, the treasure remains undetected."

Thomas smiled, his remaining teeth gleaming yellowish brown in the firelight. "You are a smart boy, Adam," he said. "I've always thought you the smartest of your father's children."

Adam dipped his head modestly, though he couldn't help thinking with amusement that Ellie would certainly have something to say about their grandfather's assessment. She was always saying that while Adam might have as much natural intelligence as she did, he used it only half as much.

"You remind me a bit of myself at your age." Thomas's watery eyes had gone distant now. "I once thought the world was mine for the taking. . . . Ah, well. Time passes." He coughed into his sleeve, then focused in on Adam again. "And time will not wait for me much longer. That's why I want to give you this."

Reaching out, he took one of Adam's hands in his own. Then he pressed the medallion into his grandson's palm.

"The medallion?" Adam looked down at it. "You're giving it to me?"

"Indeed. Do not tell your brother George—he may be hurt that I did not choose him." The old man touched his thin, dry lips. "George is a fine boy, but he is a conventional thinker. He does not have the mind, nor do I believe the drive, to decipher this secret. But perhaps you do, my boy." He let out a sigh that turned into a rattling cough. "Perhaps I should have done this sooner."

Adam could tell that this was a momentous decision for

his grandfather. He was fond of the old man and so he played along, bowing his head and thanking him with a note of proper solemnity and reverence in his voice.

However, as he climbed the narrow wooden steps to the sleeping room he shared with his brothers, he couldn't help thinking that perhaps his own father had been right to give up on the medallion. He paused on the landing to examine it by the light of his candle. The round face held a number of scratches that formed lines and rough shapes, the images worn down a bit by age and handling. It was so very, very old, more than two hundred years old now. . . . If there ever was a treasure—which seemed somewhat dubious in itself—surely it was long since lost, or found, by now.

Still, he tucked the medallion away carefully in his pocket. It might not be the key to great riches. But it was a rich reminder of his own family history, and for that reason alone it was worth treasuring.

Uncle Duncan's long, slender fingers flew over the bit of leather he was mending. Adam watched idly from his place across the table in the harness shop, the buckle he was meant to be polishing lying forgotten in his hand. His mind was wandering far afield from the dull matters of harness and horses. Talking with his grandfather the evening before had, despite his initial doubts, reawakened the old daydreams of treasure, built up and honed through the years spent listening to family stories before the fire on chilly evenings.

"Wake up, Adam!" one of his older cousins called from farther down the table. "You've been working on that single buckle for at least ten minutes."

"Oh." Adam shook off his visions of doubloons and jewels, remembering where he was. He lifted the buckle, imagining it were gold instead of brass. "Sorry."

Uncle Duncan chuckled, his bright blue eyes twinkling in his pale, narrow face. Duncan had always been a bit sickly in nature and had to walk with the aid of a cane, but he was one of the smartest men Adam knew.

"Leave your cousin alone, Will," he said. "He is a Gates man, and all Gates men require a bit of daydreaming now and again."

"Not cousin George," argued Duncan's younger son, who was soaping a harness on a rack nearby. "He never daydreams."

"True enough, and it is fitting," Duncan agreed. "For that George was named for another, a great friend of Uncle

John's and mine who was lost in the Revolution. Your cousin George is very much like him in some ways."

Just then, the shop door opened. Adam glanced up to see Ellie standing there.

"Adam," she called. "Might I speak with you a moment?"

"Of course." Relieved by even a momentary respite from his work, Adam set down his buckle and rag and hurried to join her in the stable yard just outside.

She shut the shop door carefully behind him. Now that they were standing close together in the bright afternoon sunlight, he could see that her cheeks were dotted with pink and her eyes filled with excitement.

"I have just had another letter from Private McNeal, and it gave me an idea," she told him in a low voice. "I could not wait to share it. It is the best idea I have ever had, if a bit dangerous."

"Dangerous?" Adam repeated. "What do you mean?"

She clutched him by the arm. "I want to travel south again," she said "And this time I will be sure to find Captain Lewis and volunteer to join his expedition."

If Adam hadn't known better, he might have assumed Ellie was joking. But unlike him, she rarely joked about important matters.

"Er, I see," he said. "And the private has encouraged you in this?"

"Not exactly," Ellie admitted. "He said only that it would be pleasing to see me again before he departs Philadelphia for the expedition's winter camp on one of the western rivers. But the suggestion inspired me to think more of the possibilities." She smiled eagerly. "Will you come with me, Adam? Just think of it! It would be the grandest adventure imaginable. We would be exploring an untamed land, perhaps discovering new and fantastical creatures and plants. . . ."

Adam's mind had already darted back to its earlier thoughts of treasure. What if . . . ?

But then he shook his head in disbelief. "How can you think of such a thing, Ellie?" he exclaimed. "We cannot just leave at our will for Philadelphia—let alone up and join the expedition. Mother and Father would never allow it, for one thing."

"Mother and Father would have no need of knowing until we were gone. Think of it, Adam. We could pretend we are going only as far as Sudbury to assist Aunt Mary and Cousin Eliza with the new baby, and then send word from there of our true intentions. . . ."

As Adam opened his mouth to respond, the clatter of hooves came from the entrance to the yard. Looking up, he saw a neighbor named Sims riding in with a bundle of leather tied behind his saddle.

"Gates," Sims spat out in his typical disagreeable way, "I need this lot back within the week. See to it, boy." He loosened a string, allowing the mass of harness pieces to fall to the dusty ground with a thump.

"Yes, sir," Adam muttered as the neighbor spun his horse and rode off at a trot, the animal's hooves kicking up more dust.

Staring at the mountain of sweat-marked and horse-scented harness pieces, Adam's thoughts went back to Ellie's proposed plan. True, the chances that they would be accepted for Captain Lewis's mission seemed small at best. But why not try? If what his grandfather had heard was true, they might actually have a hand at finding the Treasure of the Ancients. And at the very least it would mean another trip to the exciting and glamorous big city. If he could just arrange it somehow so that his parents wouldn't be quite so angry. . . .

"You know, you are right, Ellie," he said, the impulse overtaking him before he could stop it. He gave the pile of dirty harness a kick. "Another trip to Philadelphia might be just the thing to break up a dull summer."

Two

"Do you think George has told them yet?" Ellie asked her twin from her seat inside the coach. Her shoulder was pressed up against the window that looked out onto the driver's seat.

Adam glanced back at her from his perch behind the horses. "I imagine so," he said. "Surely he settled their minds on the matter as soon as they noticed you missing. That is why we told him, after all—so he could tell them exactly where we've gone, and why, so they will not wonder and worry."

Ellie shivered, her eyes bright and distant as she looked out at the dusty road ahead. "I can hardly believe we shall soon be in Philadelphia again."

"Yes, we should be there within the day." Adam knew how she felt. He had trouble believing it himself. Only a few weeks had passed since she first concocted her plan. They had managed to get away from home so soon only by a combination of cunning and sheer luck. A few days earlier, a man from Philadelphia who was visiting in the Concord area had fallen drunk off his horse, struck his head on a rock, and died. His connections had contacted John Gates to see about transporting his corpse back to Philadelphia via one of the Gates' carriages.

At the time he'd heard of the job, Adam had been searching his mind for a way to get himself and Ellie back to Philadelphia with the least amount of trouble possible. He had immediately seen that this dead Philadelphian was the answer. At most times he was not quick to volunteer for long journeys via horse or carriage, leaving that sort of thing to George or cousin Will. But on this occasion Adam had quickly insisted that he be the one to make the long, wearying trek to the south. His father and the others had seemed a bit surprised, but offered no argument.

Now, only a matter of miles from Philadelphia, Adam remained a bit uneasy about the whole adventure. He had always gotten along well with his father and greatly respected his mother. Had he damaged his good relations with them through this impulsive stunt?

When he glanced again at Ellie, he saw her scribbling in

her diary, not seeming to mind or even notice the jolts and jars of the carriage wheels on the rough ground. She intended to chronicle every step of this journey, as she had explained to Adam, so that she would remember it all forever.

"Do you think Father and Mother will be angry with us when we return?" he asked her.

She looked up from the diary. "Perhaps at first," she said in her straightforward way. "But do not worry, Adam. This adventure shall be worth it. Imagine what they will say when we describe our first glimpse of, say, a giant mammoth or great claw. Or when we bring them back samples of fascinating new plant life or valuable minerals."

"Or when we return bearing the Treasure of the Ancients," he added, automatically causing his sister to roll her eyes.

They had passed much of the long, dull ride down from Concord discussing the many possibilities this trip afforded them. He had been surprised by how much Ellie knew of what Captain Lewis and his recently named partner in the expedition, Captain William Clark of Kentucky, expected to discover and catalog on their journey to the West. She seemed to find the topic endlessly fascinating.

He found it interesting as well—but only to a point. Whenever he wearied of talking about the expedition, he changed the subject to other matters. Since Ellie did not like to speak of treasure-hunting, they settled on one topic they both found entertaining—codes and puzzles. They were able to divert themselves for hours on end by practicing their own coded language and by posing riddles to each other, a habit carried on since childhood when their father and grandfather would often test their minds with similar games.

"I only wish we would have told Grandfather where we were going," Adam mused now, not for the first time. "I think it would have given him great pleasure to know what we were attempting."

Ellie shot him a look. "I know," she said kindly. "But there was no chance to take him aside before we left—it all happened so fast, and we were busy figuring out how I could stow away without being detected." She chuckled. "Besides, knowing Grandfather, he would have insisted on coming along even at his advanced age, especially if you mentioned the treasure business. Just remember how tempted George was—I think if he didn't realize how much Father and Uncle Duncan count on him around the barn and livery, he might have ended up coming with us."

Adam nodded, knowing she was right but nonetheless regretting having to keep the secret from his grandfather; even more so than from his parents. Taking the reins in one hand, he reached into his pocket with the other, pulling out the wooden medallion.

"I still can't believe Grandfather gave you that." Ellie nodded toward the medallion. "You'd better never let George see it. He will be wounded that it wasn't given to him."

"I know. For some reason, Grandfather seemed determined that I should be the one to have it." Adam flipped it over in his hand, glancing down at the marks on the back side. "I don't know why. If so many generations of Gateses haven't puzzled out its meaning by now, it's surely a hopeless cause."

Ellie shrugged. She had shown little interest in the medallion either before or after it came into Adam's possession. "I suppose he thinks you are clever," she said with a sly glance. "Then again, he is very old and a bit feebleminded."

Adam chuckled and tucked the medallion away again.

"Careful, sister dear," he said. "Else you shall find yourself walking the rest of the way to Philadelphia."

"**I** cannot believe you are here!" Private Hugh McNeal had not taken his eyes off Ellie since her arrival on the doorstep of his boardinghouse, not even while he was shaking Adam's hand. "It means so much to me that you will be able to see me off on the greatest adventure of my life."

Ellie smiled and tilted her head to one side. "I hope not to have to see you off," she said. "Will you take me to Captain Lewis? I wish to offer my services, such as they are, for the good of his expedition."

McNeal hesitated. For the first time, his eyes wandered away from Ellie's own. He cleared his throat several times before answering.

"I am afraid that is impossible," he said at last. "Er, Captain Lewis is no longer in Philadelphia."

"What?" Ellie's smile faded quickly away.

"He has already left to travel to Pittsburgh, to the west," McNeal explained. "From there, he will soon be continuing even farther west to join Captain Clark at our winter camp, which lies at the mouth of the Wood River on the east side of the Mississippi, near the frontier town of St. Louis. I should be on my way there myself, but when you wrote that you were coming I simply had to stay and see you one more time."

He tentatively reached for Ellie's hand. She didn't move, her hand resting in his as limp and still as a dead fish.

"I see," she said slowly, her voice expressionless. "Well, then, I wish you bon voyage, private."

"Miss Eleanor . . ." McNeal began, clearly sensing something amiss in her expression.

"Come, Adam." Ellie's voice was tight and low. "We'd best be off."

She gathered up her skirts and strode away at top speed. Adam shot McNeal a sympathetic look and a shrug, then hurried after her. McNeal called Ellie's name a few times. But she did not respond, and Adam didn't look back again, either.

He let Ellie rush on for several blocks, knowing better than to try to stop her in such a mood. Finally, when her pace slowed a bit, he caught up and touched her on the arm. She whirled around, her eyes flashing fire.

"Can you believe this?" she cried, clasping her fists on either side of her head and shaking them. "I cannot stand it! I swear, I simply cannot stand the thought of giving up, of crawling home again to a life of ordinary dullness! Not when I was so close . . ." Her hands fell to her sides, and her voice trailed off in a sob.

Adam put an arm about her shoulders. "It will be all right," he murmured, not knowing what else to say.

He was somewhat disappointed in this turn of events himself; ever since his grandfather's comments about Lewis's expedition possibly being a treasure hunt, he'd had great fun imagining himself discovering the Treasure of the Ancients hidden in some hollow log or cave. Oh, how he would lord it over his Philadelphia cousins, who had never had to work a day in their lives! Even with such heady dreams dashed, he was nowhere near so heartbroken as Ellie appeared to be.

"Shall we return to Uncle Edward and Aunt Millicent's?" he asked gently. After dropping off their "delivery," they had left the horses and carriage at their uncle's, where they planned to stay for the remainder of their time in the city.

Ellie shook her head. "I cannot go there," she said grimly. "Not yet. Let's walk about a bit."

"All right." Adam didn't mind that at all. It was a warm but otherwise pleasant day, and he would much rather see more of the city than sit in a stuffy drawing room listening to cousin Charlotte's off-key piano scales.

"This neighborhood seems familiar." Adam looked around. "Wasn't it near here where we saw Captain Lewis back in the spring?"

"I think so," Ellie replied. After more than an hour of wandering through the streets, she seemed a bit calmer. Although, every once in a while, her cheeks flushed and her hands clenched.

Adam forgot about Lewis as he spotted a tavern sign just ahead. "Shall we stop in for a drink?" he asked. "That looks like an agreeable place, and all this walking in the hot sun has worked up a terrible thirst."

Ellie nodded and they headed for the tavern, dodging a rooting pig and a pair of ash-dusted chimney sweeps as they ducked inside. Inside, it was surprisingly airy and cool, with a number of well-dressed gentlemen and one or two ladies taking refreshment at the modest but comfortable tables. The place reminded Adam pleasantly of the similar inn run by his cousins back in Concord.

Soon he and Ellie were seated at one of the rough-hewn tables with drinks before them. "Ah, now that is better." Adam took a sip. "Everything in life seems a bit better when seen from within an amiable tavern."

"If you say so." Ellie did not seem convinced. Frown lines still marred her smooth cheeks and forehead.

"Well, look what we have here! Is it not the earnest young do-gooders I encountered in an alley near here?" a voice called out from somewhere behind Adam.

Adam glanced around for the source of the comment and saw a familiar-looking figure walking toward them from the direction of the billiards table. He gulped. It was the youngest of the Brewster brothers!

"Uh-oh," Ellie murmured, clearly recognizing the man at the same moment.

Adam tensed, remembering their last encounter and the ominous threat. But Miles Brewster remained relaxed and smiling as he approached.

"It *is* you!" he exclaimed with obvious delight. "Now, I might not have recalled *your* face, mate—" He cocked a thumb at Adam. "But I'd recognize this lovely lady any-where." Turning toward Ellie, he gave a sweeping little bow in her direction.

She smiled tightly in return. "Yes, and I certainly recall you as well, sir," she said. "I wouldn't soon forget one of three grown men who found entertainment in picking on a little boy and his mother."

Adam winced, fearing that her comment would bring forth the nasty brute he remembered from their earlier encounter. But Miles just roared with laughter.

"Aye, but she's a spunky one!" he cried, giving Adam a nudge with his elbow. "Indeed, miss, my brothers and I did have something to say to that pair, I'm afraid. The boy was, er, an old friend of ours from Washington's city, and it was an unpleasant surprise to encounter him here. But never mind that! Please allow me to reintroduce myself. . . ."

After the young man gave his own name, Adam reminded him of his and his sister's. "We are visiting once again from Concord," he explained. "We shall not be here long."

"Pleasure to make your acquaintance under more agreeable circumstances, Adam and Ellie Gates," Miles said. "My brothers and I live here in Philadelphia, but as it happens we shall not be here much longer, either. We depart in three days' time for Pittsburgh."

"Pittsburgh?" Ellie sat up straight, showing her first real

interest in the man since his approach. "Why are you going there?"

It took Adam a moment to realize the reason for her reaction. *Of course!* he thought. McNeal had mentioned Lewis was in Pittsburgh now. Ellie's mind would naturally connect the two.

Miles leaned back and propped one long arm against a nearby beam. "As a matter of fact, lovely lady, we're on an important mission," he said. "We must deliver a vital message to Captain Lewis from his good friend President Jefferson. And while we're there, we plan to offer our own services to the glorious expedition. We've heard a man might make his fortune out West." With that, he turned and gave Adam a broad wink.

Adam's heart let out a thump. Immediately, the earlier thoughts of treasure flooded his mind once again. Could Miles Brewster be alluding to the rumored search for the Treasure of the Ancients with his comments? The Brewster brothers *were* known to be treasure hunters. . . .

"Um, that *does* sound important," he said cautiously. "And I, too, have heard that there are fortunes to be made out west. As a matter of fact, I believe our two families have something in common, Mr. Brewster."

Miles raised one eyebrow. "Is that so? What might you mean?"

"We Gates men are treasure hunters as well." Adam puffed out his chest a bit, knowing that he had to impress Miles Brewster if he expected to learn anything from him. "In fact, our father is a Revolutionary War hero—through his treasure-hunting skills he discovered a vast and valuable store of munitions just before the first battle of the war. If it had not been for this discovery . . ." His voice trailed off meaningfully.

"Really?" Miles was leaning closer, looking interested.

Adam nodded. "It is true," he said. "Not only is Father a skilled and successful treasure hunter from a long line of the same, but he was well acquainted with other great men of the Revolution such as Paul Reveere and Samuel Adams. Oh, yes, the Gates name is well known and respected throughout Massachusetts."

He noticed Ellie shooting him a surprised look. And no wonder; he'd made the Gates family, famous only for good harness work in one corner of Concord, seem as renowned as President Jefferson himself. Still, judging by the look in

Miles Brewster's eye, Adam thought the exaggeration might have worked.

"Well, then," Miles said thoughtfully. "Perhaps you are right, and our families should in fact become better acquainted. How about if you and your lovely sister accompany us to Pittsburgh? I'm sure the adventure would suit a treasure hunter such as yourself. And of course I expect someone such as you, coming from one of the finest families in Massachusetts, shall have no trouble paying the coach fare west."

"That sounds like a fine adventure!" Adam said, not bothering to correct Miles's misapprehension. "I accept."

"Adam," Ellie said softly. "Are you sure? This gerstran nt-did seem ree-verr santpleas onup our last ingmeet."

"What was that, pretty miss?" Miles leaned closer, smiling insipidly at Ellie. "I didn't catch what you just said. Your voice is too soft and ladylike for a rough place like this."

"She was just fretting over the length and difficulty of the journey, as women do," Adam spoke up. "Do not worry; she shall not dissuade me."

"Very well. My brothers will be pleased to hear that

such an illustrious pair shall be joining us." Miles borrowed a scrap of paper from the tavern owner and scribbled down the information on the coach. "We shall see you in three days, then. Now I must be off to share this good news with my brothers."

After Miles had left, Adam turned to find Ellie gazing at him with troubled eyes. "Do not fret, sister dear," he said lightly. "I realize Mr. Brewster is a bit rough around the edges. But nobody expects treasure hunters to be as genteel and learned as ministers or lawyers. In any case, I don't expect you to come along. You can stay with our relatives for a while and then head home and let the family know where I've gone."

"Don't act the fool!" she replied at once, her worry replaced with irritation. "If you are off to Pittsburgh to see Captain Lewis and Captain Clark, then so am I!"

"A female explorer, eh? That's a first." Stephen Brewster let out a chortle, gazing at Ellie with his golden brown eyes. "I'd like to be there when you offer your services to Lewis."

"Laugh if you like, Mr. Brewster," Ellie said stiffly. "I

believe Captain Lewis will be willing to accept any person with knowledge and interest in his quest and an acceptance of the risks of the voyage."

"We shall see, eh?" Stephen traded a smirk with his brothers. "Mr. Gates, what shall you decide if you are accepted by the esteemed Captain Lewis and your sister is not, I wonder?"

"What matter is it? I doubt we shall have to worry over the question." Adam shifted his weight on the seat, trying to avoid the metal-bound trunk edge that had been poking him in the ribs for the past two hours. Despite their party of five being the only passengers, there wasn't much room inside the coach, as it was stuffed to the roof with packages and freight, with still more tied to the top and rear.

At that moment, the coach bounced over a rut in the road, throwing the passengers all about the place and eliciting muttered oaths from two of the Brewsters. They had only been underway a few hours, but already the road was growing rougher as they traveled away from civilization and into the vast wilderness lying between the two Pennsylvania cities.

The Gates' traveling companions were also growing

rougher as time passed. Adam had spent enough time staring at the Brewster brothers to know their faces by heart. Stephen, the eldest, was also the tallest and handsomest. He had a wiry build and a loud, commanding way about him. The middle brother, Roger, was the shortest of the trio but also the most broadly built, with bulging muscles and a hard, cruel look about his jaw and brow. Miles, the youngest, was the most talkative and least clever about hiding his thoughts and feelings—which most certainly included some tender interest toward Ellie.

Adam had hardly recovered from the jolt when he felt the carriage slow and heard the driver calling to his horses. A moment later, they were at a full stop. Peering out the window, Adam saw no settlement or any sign of civilization at all.

"What is happening?" he called out to the driver.

The driver, a stout little man with tufts of reddish brown hair over a weather-beaten face, leaned in. "Goin' to rest the horses a moment," he said in his brusque way. "Need to tie down a few things tighter up top. Be under way again in a bit."

"Very well." Adam sat back and glanced at Ellie. He was

about to ask her how she was doing, when a sudden shout went up from outside.

"What now?" Miles exclaimed, glancing out the window.

Adam was already reaching for the door. "I'll go see."

He hopped out of the coach and glanced up. The driver was standing on the front seat reaching up onto the roof.

"What is it?" Adam called. "Do you need some help?"

The driver let out an oath. "We have a stowaway!" he exclaimed. Lunging forward, he gave a yank at someone or something unseen up top.

A second later, a wiry and grungy young boy tumbled to the rocky road with an *oof.* When he rolled over and sat up, rubbing an elbow, Adam gasped.

It was the same street urchin he and Ellie had rescued from the Brewsters on their first trip to Philadelphia!

Three

"How dare ye, boy?" the driver roared, hopping down and moving toward the stowaway. "I'll have no deadheads on my coach!"

By now, the Brewsters were climbing out to see what was going on. They recognized the stowaway as quickly as Adam had.

"What have you, a death wish, you cussed little imp?" Stephen exclaimed.

Roger made a fist and pounded it into his opposite palm. He took a threatening step foward. "Indeed he must, since he has chosen to play the spy yet again."

Miles darted forward and grabbed the boy roughly by the shoulder. "He won't get away from us this time, that's for certain." He glanced around at the wild forest pressing up against the road in all directions. "And if he does, the wild beasts and savages will take care of him soon enough," he added with a smirk.

"Wait, now," Adam said, alarmed. "What ill will do you three hold toward this child, anyway?"

"That's no business of yours, Gates," Stephen snarled.

The driver shouldered Miles aside and grabbed the boy himself. "*This* is business of mine," he cried. "Let me have him!"

"Just a moment, everyone," Adam said in the most soothing manner he could muster. "Let us not proceed too hastily. Shouldn't we ask the boy why he chose to steal away on this coach?"

"Good question." The driver glared at the boy. "Answer it, boy, if you know what's good for ye!"

The boy merely returned the man's stare. He tilted his narrow chin upward a bit, apparently undaunted by the men around him.

"Here, let me have him." Stephen said. "I'll get an answer out of him one way or another."

Ellie had just climbed down from the coach behind the others. Her eyes widened when she recognized the boy. A quick glance around appeared to be all she needed to tell her what was happening.

"Here, let me try," she said, pushing her way past

the Brewsters to the driver. "Sir, if you please. It is quite obvious you are frightening him with your rough manner. Perhaps he will respond better to me."

"Frightening him?" the driver exclaimed. "Indeed I do intend to frighten him!"

"Please." Adam stepped forward, smiling and putting a hand on the man's arm. "What harm is there in my sister trying? At least then we shall know the truth of the matter, don't you agree, sir?"

The driver glared at him for a moment. Then he shrugged and stepped back. "Very well, she can try if she likes," he muttered. "But there are no deadheads allowed on my coach, mark my words."

Adam let out a silent breath of relief. Then he glanced at Ellie. She was already leading the boy away from the group by a gentle hand around his thin shoulders. He went along with her willingly, and the two of them stopped a little way down the road and leaned close together. Immediately, Ellie began talking.

"There, now," Adam said lightly. "Ellie shall get the truth out of him if anyone can."

Sure enough, his sister returned a few minutes later. The

boy trailed close behind her, but hung back warily once she'd reached the group.

"This boy is now an orphan," Ellie said, her blue eyes sad. "His mother succumbed to consumption shortly after we first saw them, and he's been on his own ever since, stranded in Philadelphia—an unfamiliar city, as he comes from Washington. Oh, and he was not following the three of you by stowing away." She shot an unfriendly look at the Brewsters. Then she sighed and glanced at the ground. "He was—he was following me," she added softly.

Adam raised his eyebrows. "He was? Why?"

"Because I was kind to him." Ellie bit her lip. "He remembered me from before. And when he spotted me again, he followed me all the way onto this coach." Her expression hardened as she looked around at the other men. "That makes me responsible for his welfare," she added, her voice now very firm. "And, as such, I must insist that none of you lay a hand on him or otherwise cause him harm."

"Indeed?" Stephen didn't seem certain whether to be annoyed or amused. "And you shall stop us, shall you, Miss Gates?"

Ellie glared at him. "Indeed I shall."

Roger grumbled a bit under his breath, but Miles cleared his throat. "Listen, boys," he said to his brothers. "It's no matter, really. The boy cannot damage us out here away from all civilization, can he?"

"It's settled, then," Adam jumped in before Miles's brothers could argue. He hadn't been looking forward to backing up Ellie against all three of the Brewsters plus the coach driver. Although why the brothers hated the boy *so* much was curious. . . .

"Is it, indeed?" The driver had been following the conversation with growing ire. Now he glared at Adam, then at the boy. "Then which among you is planning to pay this rascal's fare?"

Adam swallowed hard. He and Ellie had just enough money to get themselves to Pittsburgh and back again, with only a little extra for food and other necessities. There was no way they could pay an additional fare.

Then an idea came to him. "Sir," he said to the driver, "I have some experience with horses and coaches myself. Perhaps we can work out an exchange for the boy's fare. I can drive part of the way while you rest, and help take care of the team at stops."

The driver hesitated for a moment, as if adding up the worth of Adam's offer in his head. Finally he nodded curtly. "Very well, then," he said. "Why don't you take a shift right now? I fancy a nap."

Adam let out a sigh of relief and winked at Ellie, who was shooting him a grateful look. Then, feeling lighter of heart than he had since before the discovery of the stowaway, he turned and smiled at the boy. "What's your name, lad?" he asked.

The boy merely peered back at him suspiciously from behind Ellie. When Adam took a step toward him, he scowled and skirted backward.

Adam shrugged. "Oh, well," he said to the Brewsters, who were smirking. "I suppose it shall take a while to win him over."

"If you want to know his name, I can tell you that," Ellie spoke up. "He is Franklin Poole. His parents were immigrants. They arrived here several years ago from Ireland."

"Irish, eh?" Stephen said with a loud snort. "Explains a lot."

Ellie glared at him. "What do you mean by that?" she demanded.

"Shut up, Stephen," Miles said at the same time. "This guttersnipe isn't worth the trouble. Now let's stop arguing and get back in the coach; else we'll never reach Pittsburgh."

Adam did his best to stretch his arms within the confines of his corner of the coach. He was stiff and sore from hours of driving—the coachman had taken full advantage of Adam's offer to share his duties. Still, he wasn't at all sleepy. His mind was racing with thoughts of what would happen once they reached their destination.

"You awake?"

Adam glanced up and saw Miles looking at him. "Uh-huh," Adam said. "Looks like we're the only ones, eh?"

Indeed, the other passengers all appeared to be sound asleep. Stephen was slouched in the seat beside Adam with his hat tipped over his eyes and his long legs sprawled atop a pile of boxes. Roger was snoring loudly in the opposite corner. Next to him, Ellie was sitting up as straight as ever, but her head was tipped forward, bobbing with every movement of the coach. The boy, Franklin Poole, was curled up beside her, still as a mouse.

"Why is your sister so eager to join up with Lewis and

Clark?" Miles asked, glancing at the sleeping Ellie.

Adam shrugged. "She has always had an interest in the natural sciences," he said. "She thinks this expedition will yield many discoveries along the way. Is that not why you and your brothers wish to join?"

Miles laughed softly. "Certainly, that is what we plan to tell Captain Lewis." He shot a glance at his brothers. "But it is far from the true reason. We are sure that Lewis and Clark are not seeking scientific knowledge at all, nor trade routes or all that other rot, either. No, the real reason for this journey is that there is a vast treasure hidden somewhere in the western wilderness, and the president knows it."

"The Treasure of the Ancients?" Adam asked eagerly before he could stop himself.

Miles looked startled. "How do you know of that?"

"I told you. My family has some interest in this area." Adam shrugged. "My grandfather believes the same as you about the expedition. But how did you hear of the treasure?"

"It was my brother Roger," Miles said. "He overheard some local Freemasons talking outside their lodge—making reference to the treasure and the existence of certain clues to its location in the wilds." He pursed his thin lips. "Everyone knows that most of the important men of the government are of that brotherhood, and so when we heard of the expedition we put two and two together."

"Interesting," Adam murmured. Had his grandfather been right all along? Could there really be a great treasure hidden somewhere in the uncharted wilderness? Could that truly be the purpose behind this expedition of Lewis and Clark?

"You look a bit skeptical, Gates." Miles was watching Adam's face closely. "Don't believe me? Well, believe this. Do you recall that message my brothers and I plan to deliver to Captain Lewis? Well, we are quite certain that the letter contains the first clue to the treasure. That's why we, er, intercepted it from its original messenger while we were secretly observing the president in Washington." He shot a quick, irritated glance at the little boy in the corner of the coach.

Ah, I see, Adam thought, finally understanding the Brewsters' enmity toward the boy. *Young Franklin Poole must have witnessed this "interception" of theirs, and that is the reason they hold a grudge against him—fearing, perhaps, that he could turn them in to the authorities.*

"In any case," Miles went on, "we kept the president's message safe for him, which the first messenger failed to do." He smirked slightly. "Stephen has not let it out of his possession."

"So you plan to deliver this message to Captain Lewis when we reach Pittsburgh?" Adam asked. "Then what will you do? If, as you say, there are many clues, you will need to join the expedition. What if there is no room? And more importantly, have you figured out the meaning of the clue?"

Miles frowned, his boastful expression shutting down. "That is no business of yours," he said sharply, clearly realizing he'd said too much. "And you'll keep this to yourself if you know what's good for you. My brothers—" He shot a rather fearful glance at the two older Brewsters. "My brothers are not good at sharing."

"Do not worry. I understand their thirst for treasure very well. In fact . . ." Adam dug into his pocket, being careful not to jostle Stephen. He pulled out the medallion to show Miles. "This is the first clue to my own family's quest, one that has been passed down for generations. So you see, we have something in common, you and I."

Miles relaxed a bit as he glanced at the medallion, though he still looked wary. "That may be," he said. "But if you let my brothers know I have told you any of this . . ."

"I have no intention of telling your brothers anything at all." Adam glanced quickly at the sleeping pair. He shuddered, thinking of how they'd treated Franklin Poole and the boy knew far less detail. "Mark my word on that."

Pittsburgh was a much different kind of place than Philadelphia or Boston. Though a sizable town of some two thousand residents, with amenities that included all sorts of shops, the busy boatyards, a courthouse, and even the respectable institution of higher learning known as Pittsburgh Academy, everything about it still somehow seemed rougher and wilder than the Eastern cities, from the design of its buildings to the state of its roads to the behavior of its residents. The immense, battle-scarred Fort Pitt stood at its heart, reminding everyone who saw it that this was the frontier—the edge of the civilized world, beyond which lay miles and miles of a mysterious tangle of wilderness.

However, in some ways it was the same as anywhere. Almost before the coachman had led his weary horses to water, an acquaintance was hurrying toward him from the direction of a nearby tavern, eager for the latest word from Philadelphia on the purchase of the Louisiana Territory, the progress in the war between England and France, and other news of the day.

Adam observed all this as he gathered up their modest things from among the various baggage on the coach. He was the last of the group to disembark, immediately behind Ellie.

Franklin Poole had jumped down just ahead of her. As soon as his worn leather shoes hit the dusty ground, Stephen Brewster grabbed him by the arm.

"Now, then," he said in a silky, threatening purr. "Perhaps it is finally time to get better reacquainted."

"Remove your hand from him, sir!" Ellie said sharply. "I have told you, he is now my responsibility. If you have a quarrel with him, you have it with me."

Adam stepped down from the coach. "And me."

"Is that so?" Stephen glared at him. Roger moved a bit closer, his eyes glittering with malice.

"Stephen . . ." Miles began uncertainly, glancing from his brother to Ellie and back again.

Stephen ignored him, showing no sign of backing down until several rough-looking men loitering nearby took an interest in the scene.

"Ahoy, there." The largest of the men, who had a bristly black beard and a deep, gruff voice, stepped toward them. "I know not the custom in Philadelphia these days, but here in Pittsburgh we don't take kindly to threats against a lady and children."

Stephen let out a soft oath, and Roger's eyes narrowed. But the two of them stepped back, with Stephen dropping his hold of Franklin's arm. The boy instantly scurried to hide behind Ellie's skirts.

"We have no quarrel with you, then," Stephen said to the men. "In fact, perhaps you would do us the favor of showing us to the best place to buy a drink in this town?"

The bearded man smiled. "Indeed, that can be easily arranged, mate."

As the men hurried off, followed by the Brewsters, Adam let out the breath he hadn't realized he was holding. "Let's hope that's the last we see of those three," he said, although a small part of him could not help but think of the letter and clue in their possession. Something he would never see . . . "In any case, here we are. Should we see about securing some temporary lodgings? I also wish to send a message to Father to let him know where we are."

Ellie shook her head. "All that can wait. I want to find Captain Lewis before we miss him again."

Adam knew it was pointless to attempt debate when his sister had made up her mind, and they immediately set off with young Franklin Poole in tow. By asking passersby, they soon found their way to the docks along the Ohio River, where the town's boatbuilding trade kept things busy at all times. Once there, they were directed to a spot where there was moored a half-finished keelboat, more than fifty feet long and swarming with laborers. Standing watching the boatbuilders at work was a pale-skinned man with a long, straight nose and thin lips. He was accompanied by an immense, shaggy black dog.

"Captain Lewis, I presume?" Ellie called, hurrying toward the man.

He turned and squinted at her. "I am Captain Meriwether Lewis," he said with a bow. "How may I be of service, young lady?"

Ellie introduced herself and Adam. Then she smiled

eagerly at the young captain. "We are here because we wish to volunteer for your expedition," she said. "My brother is strong of limb, and I have much interest in the scientific discoveries that may be found out in . . ."

She trailed off when Lewis held up his hand, seeming alarmed. "Oh, my dear," he said with a brief laugh. "Of course we cannot have a woman on the expedition. It's quite out of the question!"

Four

"Oh, but, sir!" Ellie cried in dismay. "We have come all this way. . . ."

"I am very sorry, miss." Lewis's face and voice were kind, but firm. "It's just not possible." He turned and cast a glance over Adam. "Perhaps your brother could send you correspondence about the trek, however. We could use another strong young man if you're interested, son. What do you say?"

Adam hesitated, sorely tempted. The coach driver had turned out to be a gruff but principled man in the end, and Adam would trust him to carry Ellie safely back to Philadelphia should he decide to accept Captain Lewis's offer.

If the treasure is out there, I should love to be among the group that finds it, he thought, his hand wandering unbidden to touch the medallion in his pocket. *Father and Grandfather would be thrilled if I were to finally live out the old family dreams in such a way.*

It might even be enough to make them forgive me for sneaking off like this and exposing Ellie to such dangers.

But the moment he glanced at Ellie's disconsolate face, he knew he couldn't do it. This expedition was *her* dream, not his. He couldn't steal it from her. All the treasure in the world wouldn't be enough to make him forgive himself for that.

"I'm sorry," he told Lewis. "I cannot go without my sister. If you won't have her, I'm afraid you cannot have either of us."

"Fair enough." Lewis shrugged. "Good day to you both. I must go now and deal with those incorrigible drunkards who claim to be boatbuilders. . . ." Muttering under his breath, he hurried toward the half-finished barge with the big, black dog padding at his heels.

"Well, there it is, then." Adam turned to find both Ellie and Franklin Poole staring at him. He'd nearly forgotten the young boy was still around. "I suppose we'd better see about those lodgings, and then reserve a spot on the next coach back to the East."

Ellie frowned, looking as though she wanted to argue. But then she glanced out toward Captain Lewis, who was waving his arms and haranguing some of the workmen. With a sigh, she nodded.

"And what about young Frank?" Ellie asked, glancing at the boy. "We shall need to come up with the fare for him to go back with us."

"Shall we?" Adam shrugged.

Ellie narrowed her eyes at him. "What do you mean? We cannot leave him here!"

"He has no family in Philadelphia or anywhere else, except perhaps Ireland," Adam pointed out with what he thought was flawless logic. "Why should we pay an expensive fare back east when he could be equally at home anywhere? We should at least inquire as to whether Pittsburgh has an orphanage."

He glanced toward Franklin Poole—or, rather, where the boy had been a moment earlier. Now, he was gone.

Ellie looked over at the same moment. "Frank?" she called. "Where are you? Frank! Answer me, please!"

There was no response. "Come on," Adam said to Ellie. "He can't have gone far."

But their search turned up no sign of the boy. It was as if he'd vanished into thin air.

"We might as well give up," Adam said at last. "We'll never find him if he doesn't wish to be found. Unlike buried treasure, young boys don't stay in the same place and wait to be discovered. He heard our plans—if he wishes to be part of them, he'll make that known sometime before the coach leaves town."

Ellie sighed, looking troubled. "I suppose you're right." She glanced around, her brow furrowed with concern. "I only hope he stays out of sight of those Brewsters as well as he's stayed out of ours."

They left the dock area and wandered back to the main part of town. After stopping at a boardinghouse long enough to secure a room for the night, they continued on to the area where they'd left the coach.

Adam quickly arranged to reserve two spots on the next coach east, which left in two days. But when he reached into his bags to check that he had enough for the fare, he made a terrible discovery.

"Our money," he cried in horror. "It's gone!"

"Are you sure? Let me check." Ellie rushed forward, digging into the bag herself. But aside from one stray half-cent coin, there was not a shilling to be found within.

Adam put a hand to his forehead. "How could this have happened?" he moaned. "I know it was there when we left Philadelphia. Blazes! Do you suppose your little friend Frank Poole pinched it during the journey?"

"I suspect it's far more likely to have been *your* friends the Brewsters," Ellie said with a frown. "This is what you get for bragging as you did back in Philadelphia—you made our family sound terribly wealthy while you were going on about all that treasure business. No wonder Miles Brewster invited us along. Surely his only intention was to rob us. We're only lucky he and his brothers didn't make off with our shoes and clothes as well as our money!"

Adam shook his head. "What use would famous treasure hunters have with our paltry fortune? I'm sure it was Poole—he certainly seems the shifty type. But no matter. Either way, we need to figure out what to do." He hesitated. "Should we—should we send a message to Father and Mother by the next coach asking for help? Or perhaps to Uncle Edward?"

It was certainly the most sensible plan under the circumstances. The Gates family wasn't wealthy, but did well enough that they would almost certainly be able to send fare money by return coach without too much trouble. And of course Uncle Edward could easily afford to pay their fares twice over, though with the additional cost of a long lecture on responsibility at the end of it.

Ellie bit her lip. "I'm not sure I can bear the thought of begging our family to help us after sneaking off as we did," she admitted. "It would make me feel too much the fool. Is there no other way?"

Despite the grim situation, Adam couldn't help smiling. "There *is* another way," he said, some of his adventurous spirit seeping back already. He glanced around, taking in the rough, thrilling sights, sounds, and smells surrounding them. Pittsburgh might not have the cosmopolitan charms and amenities of Philadelphia or Boston, but it was still a new place worth exploring. Something neither Gates twin would pass up.

"What is it, then?" Ellie asked. "Shall we have to sell our teeth to some local dentist to make our fare home?"

Adam ran his tongue over his teeth. "I think not," he assured her. "We are both young and strong; surely I'll have no trouble finding work in one of the local stables—that should pay sufficiently to cover our rooms with enough left over that it shouldn't take more than a month or two to save enough for our fares back home."

Ellie nodded, her expression brightening slightly. "And perhaps I can find work as a stable hand as well, or even as a seamstress if necessary."

"There you have it." Adam grinned at her. "This way, we shall get a bit of adventure in Pittsburgh, after all, even if it's not precisely the adventure we originally sought."

The weeks passed, and the weather grew colder as summer faded into autumn and then early winter. As predicted, Adam's horse-keeping skills had made it easy for him to find work, though the pay was somewhat lower than he'd been expecting. Ellie, too, was able to find odd jobs here and there. In this way, they kept up with the cost of their cramped but clean rooms and paid for their meals and other necessities. They had sent word to their family letting them know of their whereabouts, and had since received several letters in return. It was difficult to tell from mere words on paper just how their impulsive adventure was viewed back home, but Adam figured they could deal with that in person once they returned.

One early December day, Adam returned from work to find Ellie staring out the window. "What is it?" he asked, stomping the snow off his shoes. "You have an odd look about you."

"I met with Private McNeal."

At that, Adam stopped short in surprise. "McNeal? I thought he was long gone," he repeated. "How did you come to meet with him?"

"He arrived in Pittsburgh this morning. He will be leaving to join Captain Lewis and Captain Clark at their winter camp this week."

Adam nodded. Lewis had left Pittsburgh soon after their meeting in August, just as soon as his keelboat was finished. Ellie hadn't mentioned it much since then, but Adam suspected that she still thought often of how much she wished to be with him, preparing for the grand adventure ahead.

"Come," Adam said, wishing to distract her from such thoughts if possible. "Let us seek out our evening meal at the tavern tonight."

Soon the two of them were seated in the closest tavern. Ellie cheered up a little once she had food before her. They were speaking of their progress on saving enough to get home—though at this point, with the season's first snow already on the ground, they expected to wait out the winter in Pittsburgh—when there came the sound of heavy footsteps approaching the table.

"Well, look who we have here, boys."

Adam winced, instantly recognizing Stephen Brewster's sardonic voice. Glancing up, he saw the brothers standing there staring down at him.

"Good evening, fellows," Adam said mildly. "I did not know you were still in Pittsburgh."

"Yes, we are still in Pittsburgh." Stephen leaned down and rested his hands on the table, glaring from Adam to Ellie and back. "Thanks to the two of you!"

"Whatever do you mean?" Ellie asked with a frown.

"He means Captain Lewis wouldn't have us," Miles spoke up. "Said our reputation preceded us—whatever that means."

"We know what it means," Roger growled. "It means someone has a big mouth."

"Right. Someone *besides* our youngest brother, you mean." Stephen turned his glare briefly on Miles, who stared down sheepishly at his feet. Then he returned his ire to the Gates twins. "Yes, I know that Miles blabbed to you about this." He yanked a sheet of paper out of his breast pocket and waved it in front of Adam. "But if you know what's good for you, you'll forget you ever heard a word about it."

"Of course," Adam replied automatically.

But his eyes were following the paper with great curiosity. He had just caught a glimpse of its contents. He could not be positive, of course, after such a brief view, but it appeared that the letter consisted of nonsense words. Could the message from the president to Lewis be in code?

As soon as the brothers had moved on, he told Ellie about his conversation with Miles months ago and what he had seen just now. "Isn't that interesting?" he finished, shooting a glance at the brothers. "I wonder if they've been able to decode the message."

"I do not care about that." Ellie glanced at the Brewsters as well, a disapproving frown on her face. "But if they stole that letter, as Miles seemed to imply in what he told you, someone should alert the president. Especially since it appears that they now have no intention of passing it on to its rightful recipient, after all."

Adam nodded. "You are right," he said. "If that had been their intention they would have done so upon approaching Lewis. Perhaps we shall try to get a message to the president when we return east. In the meantime . . ." He sneaked one more peek at the trio who were laughing in the far corner. "It might be better not to mention such things too loudly around here, in order to avoid further confrontation with the Brewsters."

Fortunately, after that encounter the Brewster brothers seemed to disappear for good, and were seen no more in Pittsburgh. And Adam, for one, was very glad about that.

Five

Adam opened the front of his coat, allowing the night air to envelop him. Even though the sun had set, the air was warm with a hint of the coming spring. He had spent another long day working at the local stable, though he expected it would be one of his last. He and Ellie had saved enough between them by now to pay their fare back home. It had taken longer than expected, but with luck, they would be back in Concord by May. Adam was looking forward to seeing his family and friends again, along with the familiar sights and activities of home. Even fixing a harness no longer seemed quite as dull as it once had, especially after so many months spent cleaning out stalls and hauling water.

Still, it is too bad that we must head back with nothing to show for it, he thought. *So much for the grand and rich adventure we imagined. . . .*

For a moment, his mind returned to Captain Lewis's offer. Where would he be right now had he accepted? Down the river at the group's winter camp, perhaps, preparing to embark upon the journey of a lifetime. Or finding the first signs of vast riches?

Nevertheless, it did no good to think of that, or of the Brewsters' quest for treasure, which often flashed through his mind. Had they decoded that message yet? Somehow he doubted it. While the brothers had a sort of wily cleverness about them, it was hard to imagine any of them having the wit to interpret any cipher that a man as learned as President Jefferson might invent.

Perhaps Miles could manage it, Adam thought as he walked, his feet carrying him through the now familiar streets and alleys of Pittsburgh. *He seems a bit more intelligent than the older two. I only wish I'd had a better look that evening in the tavern—from that brief glimpse it appeared most likely to be a simple substitution cipher, and I am sure I could work it out if I could see the whole thing. . . .*

Suddenly he had the unsettling feeling that he was being watched. He was not sure what it was that had brought about that impression, but the feeling was immediate and inescapable. Glancing around, he saw no one within view aside from a cat crossing the street half a block back. Was it his imagination, or was he being followed?

He kept walking at the same pace, but now his mind was

racing. As he had just been thinking about the Brewsters, his first suspicion was that one of them was playing games with him. Neither Adam nor Ellie had seen or heard news about them since that last encounter in the tavern back in December; for all Adam knew, they could have been laying low in Pittsburgh all winter hoping to stay out of sight and out of mind while they tried to figure out the clue. What if they had returned now to find him? After all, he had bragged enough to Miles of his treasure-hunting skills; perhaps they had finally decided that they needed his help and were coming after him now to procure it by any means necessary.

Adam's steps grew quicker and all his senses were on alert. Was that the soft breathing of a pursuer, or merely the grunt of a sleeping pig or dog in the alley? He glanced from side to side as he walked; a few steps later he caught a flash of movement out of the corner of his eye.

I see, he thought with a twinge of amusement mixed with irritation. *So that is how it is. Perhaps two can play at this game. . . .*

Keeping his pace steady, Adam waited until the last possible moment and then ducked down a handy alleyway between two buildings. He broke into a run, jumping over trash, puddles, and a sleeping dog and then rounding the corner, where he pressed himself against the wall and waited with bated breath, straining to hear if anyone was coming up behind him.

He had almost decided to give up, thinking his pursuer had gone a different way, when he heard it: the almost imperceptible pad of bare feet against the ground. Holding his breath, he kept still. A moment later a small, slim figure crept into view. Leaping forward, Adam grabbed Franklin Poole—for it was he—by the shoulder.

"You!" he cried, holding the struggling boy at arm's length to avoid the blows from his wildly waving fists and feet. "Why are you following me?"

The boy did not answer, merely glaring at Adam with fierce dark eyes. Franklin Poole had not been the picture of respectability the last time Adam had seen him, but now he appeared nearly feral. His black hair was shaggy and long, his clothes ragged, his pointy-chinned face darkened by the elements.

"Not feeling talkative today, eh? That's a real change." Noticing that one of the boy's fists clutched a bit of dirty paper, Adam reached for it. "What have you there?"

He twisted the paper free of the small, grungy hand, eliciting another glare. Glancing down, he first thought it only a collection of meaningless lines and crudely drawn figures. Then he blinked as he noticed that the drawing looked oddly familiar. . . .

"Where did you get this?" he exclaimed. "It matches the etching on my medallion! But how did you—I never showed you that, did I?"

"Out in the woods," Franklin blurted out abruptly, his voice tinged with the lilt of a brogue. He frowned. "Saw it there."

"Out in the woods?" Adam echoed, perplexed. He was so confused that he loosened his grip on the boy. Sensing his opportunity, Franklin immediately twisted his arm and broke free, disappearing back down the alley. "Hey! Wait, come back! I'm not going to . . ." Adam ran a few steps after the boy, but then stopped and sighed. It would be a hopeless chase in the dark. ". . . hurt you," he finished, knowing the boy was long gone and could not hear him.

Ah, well, he thought. *At least now I know the boy is still alive. That should make Ellie feel better, in any case.*

He glanced down again at the rough drawing in his

hand. Out in the woods . . . What could it mean? How had the image from his medallion come to be on this paper, and *where* had Frank gotten it?

"Hurry." Adam stood in the doorway of Ellie's room at the boardinghouse, glancing back as she tucked a handful of letters into one of her bags. "We do not want to be late for the coach."

Ellie glanced up. "Do not fret," she said. "We have plenty of time."

Adam knew she was right. The coach was not scheduled to leave Pittsburgh for several hours yet, and the two of them had already reserved their spots. But he couldn't help feeling a strange sort of restlessness as they prepared to depart. He supposed it was because he was alternately anticipating and dreading their return to Concord. Perhaps in the end their extended stay in Pittsburgh had not been the kind of experience that men wrote books or plays about. But it had been a change from Adam's ordinary life, one he hadn't anticipated, and he had enjoyed it for that reason alone.

While he still looked forward to seeing the rest of his family again, the closer that moment came, the more he wondered what they would have to say. Surely his mother would scold him for endangering himself and Ellie, and George would be disapproving and complain of the extra work he'd had in his absence. Then there was their father. Would he forgive his children's thirst for adventure? Or would he be disappointed that Adam had not taken the opportunity for the much-greater adventure that Lewis had offered him?

It took him a few moments to realize that Ellie was still puttering about in the flat. "What is it?" he asked impatiently. "Are you not ready to go yet?"

Ellie frowned. "Forgive me, brother." Her tone was rather sharp. "But perhaps I am not so eager as you are to give up my dreams entirely and crawl home in defeat."

Adam sighed. If only she knew . . . "You've had another letter from McNeal, haven't you?" The young private had been writing to Ellie with great regularity all through the winter. Every time one of his letters arrived, Ellie spent the next few days short-tempered and out of sorts. Adam guessed that any news of the expedition only served to remind her that she was not to be a part of it.

"Never mind that," Ellie snapped now. "What about

young Frank? Now that you've seen him, how can we just abandon him here on his own?"

Adam shook his head. "I wish I'd never told you about seeing him last week," he grumbled, only half in jest. He had discussed his encounter with the boy with his sister, and showed her the drawing. Ellie hadn't had any more idea than he about what it might mean, nor could she deduce why the same image would appear here—in the middle of the wilderness.

"At the very least, we could take one more look around for him," Ellie said, breaking into his thoughts. "Where is the harm in that? We have no better way to pass the time until the coach departs."

"All right, if you insist." Adam knew better than to argue with his twin in her current mood. Still, he couldn't help wondering what exactly they would do with the boy if they did find him. They had money enough for two fares, but not three. As it was, they were counting on their uncle's help to get them from Philadelphia back to Concord. And somehow, Adam didn't think he'd be able to talk another coach driver into carrying Franklin all that way for free.

Lugging their belongings, the twins left the boardinghouse and wandered down the street. Ellie walked ahead, calling out Franklin's name every few steps. Adam drifted along behind her, lost in his own thoughts.

All around me, exciting things are happening, he thought. *Thanks to President Jefferson, Mr. Monroe, Mr. Livingston, and the others, this country has just doubled in size. Lewis and Clark are preparing to set out and map the new territory on their way to the western sea. The Brewster brothers may be on the track to discovering a treasure for the ages, or at least giving it a good try. Even Franklin Poole is out there exploring and making mysterious drawings and doing who knows what else.*

He thought of that rough little sketch now tucked away in his pocket. If he left Pittsburgh now, he might never figure out what it meant. His steps slowed nearly to a stop, allowing Ellie to get nearly half a block ahead.

And what am I doing? he thought with a grimace. *Riding back to Concord to return to my life of repairing harnesses, shoveling manure, and listening to my father and grandfather and uncle tell tales of glory from when they were my age . . .*

He was startled out of such morose thoughts by a shriek from just ahead. Glancing forward, he gasped in horror. The Brewster brothers had just leaped out of a nearby doorway. Stephen and Miles had grabbed Ellie, one holding each of her arms while she struggled and kicked and cried out.

"Ellie!" Adam shouted, dropping his bags and racing ahead.

But Roger Brewster stepped forward, blocking his path. He was holding a stout tree branch in one strong hand.

"Adam!" Ellie screamed as the two men dragged her back toward the doorway.

"I'm coming!" Adam cried.

Roger's lips stretched into a nasty smile. "No," he growled. "You're not."

He swung the branch at Adam. Adam tried to duck, but he wasn't fast enough. The branch connected solidly with his head; he heard a hollow, oddly distant-sounding *thwack*, and his mind exploded into pinpoint lights, like a shower of sparks after a log was thrown on the fire.

Then everything went black.

Six

Adam came to with a gasp, his head throbbing with pain. It took much more than the usual effort to open his eyes. When he finally managed it, it didn't do him much good; the lighting was murky and all he could see was a rough wooden wall with a single window high up in it. He tried to get to his feet, but found himself hindered by tight, scratchy ropes about his wrists and ankles, which caused him to fall off the chair where he had been propped up and land with a thud on the puncheon floor.

"Adam! Are you all right?"

Recognizing his sister's anxious voice coming from somewhere behind him, Adam twisted his neck and shoulders until he could see her. This also allowed him to see the rest of the room he was in. It was small and dingy, littered with half-eaten food and other debris and lit only by a single candle.

"Awake again, are we?" Miles Brewster appeared out of the shadows. He strode over, grabbing Adam by the arm and hoisting him back upright into his chair after turning it to face in toward the main part of the room. Then Miles glanced over at Ellie, who had taken a few steps toward them. "Now sit yourself back down, darling," he instructed, nodding at a chair that looked identical to the one Adam found himself in. "Or I'll have to tie you back up."

"Do not tell me what to do, you incorrigible scoundrel!" Ellie cried, clenching her fists at her sides. Her hair had come loose from the usual knot she wore it in and fell about her shoulders. One cheek was smudged with dirt, but she appeared otherwise unharmed and unbowed.

Miles laughed and shook his finger in her direction. "Now, now," he warned. "Do not forget that you have me to thank for your lives, Miss Gates. So far, that is. I can't guarantee I'll be able to restrain my brothers for long if you should start causing a ruckus."

"Ellie," Adam croaked out uncertainly. His mind felt as if it were stuffed with cotton, and he was having trouble keeping up with what was happening. "Where are we?"

"The Sterbrew thersbro have kentay us onerpris," Ellie said. "They pectex us to—"

"Enough!" Miles snapped. "I'll hear no more of your

coded talk unless you wish me to immediately return your brother to unconsciousness." To illustrate his threat, he reached for an iron bar propped up against the wall nearby.

"No, no!" Ellie cried. "I shall stop."

Adam shook his head, trying to banish the fuzziness around the edges of his mind. "Why have you abducted us in this way? What harm have we done to you?"

"It is very simple, my friend." Miles stepped closer, peering at him. "While my brothers and I were away down the river this winter—"

"They were spying on Lewis and Clark," Ellie put in disapprovingly. "I heard them talking of it earlier."

"Silence!" Their captor lifted the iron bar, waving it in Adam's general direction. Ellie fell silent once again, though with a hint of mulishness in her eyes. "Now, then," Miles continued. "As I was saying, I mentioned that medallion of yours that you showed me once and told them about your family's illustrious past. My brothers were most interested at hearing of it." He smirked. "They are examining it even as we speak in the other room. They hope it could be the clue we need to the great treasure we are seeking."

Adam's hand twitched, trying vainly to reach the pocket

where he'd kept the medallion. Even as the main part of his mind was trying to imagine how they might escape this predicament, another part insisted on working out what this meant in terms of the treasure quest. If the Brewsters had returned in search of his medallion, it indicated they'd made little progress over the winter with their letter. Why else would they care about his treasure?

That gave him an idea. "Ah, I can see that you are more clever than I thought—indeed the quest I referred to that day in the coach is that for the Treasure of the Ancients," he lied impulsively. "But the medallion won't do you any good. Not without me. For I am the only one who knows how to interpret it."

Ellie glanced over at him in surprise. Miles narrowed his eyes. "You wouldn't lie to me, would you, Gates?" He grabbed Adam by the shoulder and glared into his face, so close that Adam could easily detect the sour scent of chewing tobacco on his breath. Then he abruptly let him go. "I'll have to see what my brothers think of this," he muttered. Digging some rope out of a pile of trash, he grabbed Ellie. "Quiet!" he ordered when she squealed in protest. "Now both of you will sit tight until we decide what to do."

He tied up Ellie with the rope, then stalked out of the room, slamming the door behind him. A moment later the sound of all three brothers' voices came from the next room.

Adam couldn't quite hear their words, though their tone expressed something between annoyance, excitement, and frustration. "Can you hear anything?" he hissed at Ellie, who was closer to the door.

She scooted her chair a little closer and cocked her head. "It sounds as if they are deciding what to do," she whispered back after a moment. She paused. "They are not sure whether to believe you, or to kill you, or perhaps— perhaps to kill me to convince you to tell them all you know."

Adam winced. He was already regretting his impulsive lie. It seemed all it had done was buy them a few minutes, with perhaps an even worse outcome in the end.

He jumped as a scraping sound came from somewhere behind him. Both he and Ellie turned to see what had caused it, and gasped in unison.

"Frank!" Ellie exclaimed. "Can it really be you?"

Adam could only stare in speechless amazement, wondering if this was some trick of his mind resulting from the blow to his head. For surely that couldn't be Franklin Poole clambering into the room through its single small window, a knife clenched between his teeth.

The boy dropped lightly to the floor. "I saw them," he said in his high-pitched voice, moving toward Ellie with nary a glance for Adam. "I saw them take you, Miss Ellie. Be still, and I'll cut you loose right quick."

It was more words than Adam had ever heard the boy string together at once. Ellie smiled at the boy gratefully. "Release Adam first, Frank," she urged softly.

Franklin hesitated halfway between the pair, knife held at the ready. He glanced at Adam with distaste. "No, I shall do you first, miss," he said.

"Please, Frank." Ellie's voice was kind but insistent. "If you help Adam now, then he can help you release me and we can all be away before they come back."

Franklin still looked unconvinced. But he nodded, turning and racing over to Adam. "Be still," he hissed his voice decidedly less friendly than when he'd been talking to Ellie. "Else I'll cut you."

Adam wasn't sure whether that was a warning or a threat. Either way, he stayed as motionless as possible as the boy set to work on the ropes about his wrists. The knife nicked his skin a time or two, but Adam only bit his lip and didn't make a peep.

Before long, the ropes were frayed enough for Adam to pull away and twist his hands free. "Here, give me the knife," he whispered, grabbing it before the boy could protest. Then he bent over, his shoulders stiff from their confinement, and began sawing at the ropes around his ankles.

"Hurry!" Ellie whispered. "I think I hear them coming back."

"Give me the knife!" Franklin exclaimed softly, making a move to snatch it back.

Adam evaded him easily. "Stop it!" he hissed. "Just a moment more, and then we can free Ellie and be out of here."

With that, the last fibers of the rope snapped and his legs were free. Springing to his feet, he tried to leap across the room toward his sister but almost fell—his feet and lower legs had been tied so tightly for so long that they now refused to obey his commands. The momentary distraction of all this allowed Franklin to dart in and grab the knife.

"Keep still, Miss Ellie," the boy said eagerly. "I'll just—"

At that moment the door swung open, revealing all three Brewster brothers. "What's all this, then?" Stephen roared.

"Away!" Ellie cried. "Run, Frank. Adam! Get out before they kill you!"

The feeling was coming back in Adam's feet by now. He hesitated, his heart racing with panic, not knowing what to do. When Ellie shrieked out once more for him to go, he sprang into action, obeying her command. Franklin was already scrambling out through the window with the help of Adam's chair, and Adam followed. The window was barely large enough for him to squeeze through, and he left behind several bits of skin from his arms and torso as he wriggled through it. He was almost out when he felt someone grab his right ankle. Kicking out in a panic, he felt his foot connect painfully with something. A howl went up, and his ankle was free.

He fell to the ground and quickly scrambled to his feet. Seeing Franklin racing off ahead of him, he followed. Angry shouts came from behind them, and a moment later the sharp retort of a Brown Bess rang out. Just ahead, Adam saw the lead bullet rip into the wall of a building. The Brewsters were shooting at them!

Seven

"This way!" Franklin shouted from just ahead.

Not knowing what else to do, Adam raced after the boy as he led the way down a narrow, twisting alley and out the other side. For the next few minutes they zigzagged here and there, dodging from one alley, building, or clump of trees to another and at one point even hiding behind a small herd of loose cows. At first, the sounds of running feet and the occasional musket shot followed close behind, but those sounds eventually grew more distant and then faded out altogether. It was only then that Franklin stopped running, skidding to a stop in a sheltered spot near the wall of Fort Pitt.

Adam collapsed onto the ground beside him, panting and red-faced, his aching head spinning. "Ellie!" he croaked out painfully, his throat constricting with terror. Now that the immediate panic has passed, it had been replaced with a growing sense of dismay. How could he have left his sister behind with those thugs?

Franklin seemed to be entertaining the same thoughts. He glared at Adam with intense hate that Adam scooted away from the boy.

"Knew I shoulda cut her free first," Franklin muttered.

Adam climbed to his feet. He felt guilty enough as it was without Franklin adding to it, and was tempted to chase him off. But he stopped himself, knowing that Ellie would want him to do his best to keep the boy safe. Besides, Franklin *had* rescued him. That somehow made him seem his responsibility—like it or not.

"Come along," he growled, grabbing Franklin by one thin arm. "Let's get away from here until I can figure out what to do."

Ignoring the boy's protests, he dragged him along as he headed for the relative safety of a busier part of town. Soon he was wandering the streets near the docks, desperately trying to devise a plan to save Ellie from her captors.

It was only a short while later that he saw Miles Brewster approaching through the crowds of shoppers, laborers, and others wandering about. With so many people around and Miles appearing unarmed, Adam felt confident enough to step forward to meet him.

"Where's my sister?" he demanded.

"There you are," Miles said calmly. "Bet you think you're clever, don't you?" He noticed Franklin and his lip twisted in a sneer. "It figures the guttersnipe is involved in this mess."

Adam let go of Franklin's arm. "Never mind him," he said. "Is Ellie all right? What will it take to make you release her? I'll give you all the money we have in exchange for her freedom."

Miles ignored the desperate offer. "I have a message from my brothers," he said. "If you tell us the meaning of the medallion, we'll return your sister. If not, well . . ." He smirked. "Let's just say it would be in her best interest if you cooperate."

Adam's head was spinning with panic. He had been bluffing before; not only did the medallion have nothing whatsoever to do with the Treasure of the Ancients as far as he knew, he had no more idea of its meaning than anyone else. His entire family had spent generations trying to figure it out, with no luck. What was he supposed to say now?

One thing was certain—he couldn't admit the truth.

Ellie's life depended on it. "Er, all right," he said, thinking fast. "You've heard that the Treasure of the Ancients was hidden at the end of a trail of clues, right?"

Miles nodded. "Go on."

"Well, the medallion is meant to be the first clue." Adam's mind raced, trying to concoct a likely seeming tale. "The markings on it make a map. It shows the river here—" He waved a hand at the Ohio nearby. "And the arrow on the side and the six slash marks across the central figure show that you must travel downstream until you spy a mountain range with six peaks, then find the oldest building in the nearest settlement there. It, er, it will be marked with—er, with another map that you must follow to the treasure."

Miles was listening carefully. "Very well," he said, when Adam finished. "I'll go tell my brothers what you've said, and if they're satisfied, we'll deliver Ellie to you by the north wall of the fort within the hour."

"All right. I shall wait there." Adam felt limp with relief. It had worked! He felt a flash of regret and mortification knowing he'd surely lost that medallion to the Brewsters for good. But if all went well, he and Ellie could still make that coach back to Philadelphia—and be long gone before the brothers realized that story he'd just told Miles was nothing more than a tall tale.

Realizing that he still needed to figure out what to do about Franklin, he glanced around. There was no sign of the boy.

Oh, well, Adam thought with a twinge of guilt. *Perhaps he just slipped away for the moment because he was frightened of Miles. If he comes back, I'll figure out what to do about him then.*

Adam squinted at the position of the sun. The promised hour had come and gone. And still there was no sign of Ellie.

He pushed away from the fort's thick wall and paced back and forth, feeling helpless and uncertain. It was clear by now that the Brewsters had no intention of honoring their deal. So what should Adam do now? He was no coward, and had welcomed his share of fights and roughhousing throughout his boyhood. The impulsive part of him wanted to rush back to the Brewsters' rooms and battle his way to Ellie. Or go to the authorities . . .

But the more rational part of his mind knew that that would be foolish. There were three of the Brewsters to one of him. Besides, they clearly had at least one firearm at their disposal, while he had only his fists. And he had no idea if the authorities would think this situation worth following up on.

Still, he couldn't just wait there until nightfall like some simpleton. Finally, he hit upon another plan. He would sneak back to their rooms and try to get a glimpse of Ellie through the window. Perhaps he could also spy enough to get a sense of what the Brewsters intended to do next, and plot his own next move from there.

He felt better as soon as he had a plan, vague though it might be. Leaving the fort behind, he hurried back through the maze of streets until he found the house he had exited so hastily hours earlier. Once there, he watched for a few moments from a doorway across the street until reasonably certain none of the Brewsters were standing sentry or looking out the windows. Then he stole over to the building.

When he looked in the window through which he'd escaped, he saw that the room was empty, only the over-turned chair and the iron pipe showing that he had the right spot. Moving carefully down the wall, he made his way toward another window that should show him the next room. But when he looked in, that room was empty as well. Where were the Brewsters? And more importantly, what had they done with Ellie?

Just then, he heard a soft whistle from nearby, like a bird in song. Glancing over, he spotted Franklin lurking in the shadows of the next building. The boy darted toward him, his face as unfriendly as ever.

"She's not here no more," Franklin said. "I followed him after your meeting. He came back here, and they took her."

"What?" Adam grabbed the boy by the collar, fighting back the urge to shake him. "What do you mean? Who did you follow? They took Ellie where?"

"I'm telling you, all right?" The boy looked irritated as he shook off Adam's hands. "I was watching. They didn't see me. I followed them all the way to the docks."

"The docks? They took Ellie to the docks? Why?"

Franklin shrugged. "Don't know. I came back here looking for you. I figured you'd show up when they didn't meet you."

"Come on." Adam turned to run back the way he'd come. "We've got to hurry!"

The trip to the riverside was short, though it felt to

Adam that it took a coon's age to get there. His lungs were bursting by the time he and Franklin reached the busy dock area.

"There!" Franklin cried, pointing.

Adam spun around. Stephen and Miles were aboard a small keelboat. Miles was adjusting the sails while Stephen watched Roger muscle a protesting and clearly irritated Ellie on board. A few bystanders were glancing toward the ruckus curiously, but none made a move to intervene.

"Ellie!" Adam shouted.

She jerked her head around. "Adam!" she cried.

"Blazes," Stephen swore loudly, immediately stepping over to assist Miles. "Get her on here, Roger, and let's be off!"

Adam raced toward them. Freshly cut lumber, coils of rope, and other supplies seemed to leap out at every step to block his path. He tripped over some tools once and went flying facedown onto the road, splitting open his lip. But he scrambled back to his feet and kept going. His lungs were bursting as he finally neared the Brewsters' dock.

But he was too late. The line had been loosed, and the boat was already bobbing out into the open water of the

Ohio River, the breeze filling its sails.

"Ellie!" Adam yelled, racing on, ready to make a wild leap for the departing vessel.

"Ho, boy!" A burly laborer reached out and grabbed him, hauling him back from the edge of the dock. "You're too late. They're already gone."

"I need a boat," Adam cried, struggling against the man. "Can you take me? Who has a boat? Someone must take me after them right now!"

The laborer shrugged and wandered off. Everyone else within earshot ignored his pleas, most simply moving on about their business.

Finally, Adam slumped in defeat, turning his gaze back toward the river. The laborer was right; it was too late. The boat was already moving swiftly down the river with Ellie aboard.

Eight

Adam stared after the keelboat until it was out of sight. When he could see no sign of it on the horizon, he turned to find Franklin glaring at him accusingly.

"We're too late," Adam said unnecessarily. "Why couldn't you have come to fetch me sooner? Then we might have stopped them."

"They didn't trust your story," the boy said, not bothering to respond to Adam's accusations. "Heard 'em talking. They said they was going to take her with until they saw it was real. Insurance, the tall one said." He glowered at Adam, but then his small face crumpled. "They won't hurt her, will they?"

Adam blinked. *He really is quite fond of my sister, isn't he?* he thought with some wonder. The boy might be prickly and strange, but clearly not without all human feeling.

But this was no time to ponder Franklin's temperament. Adam started pacing back and forth on the dock, his mind flitting about like a restless bird as it tried to make some sense of the situation. He had to do something to save Ellie. But what approach offered the best chance of success? Did it make more sense to use their coach fare to hire a boat to go after the Brewsters immediately? But then what would he do if he managed to catch up to them? Perhaps his efforts *would* be better spent contacting the local sheriff and seeking his assistance. . . .

Suddenly, he became aware that Franklin was poking at his arm. "What is it?" Adam exclaimed distractedly, shaking him off. "Give me a moment, I'm trying to think."

"But I got to tell you something," Franklin said.

"In a moment." Adam strode off, trying to lose the boy, at least for the moment. He was busy gauging how long it might take to track down the sheriff versus convincing one of the local boatmen to follow the three scoundrels. Would the money he and Ellie saved be enough to make it worth their while?

"Listen!" Franklin said again, his voice more urgent. "I have something here I got to show you!"

With some irritation, Adam thought back to the days when the boy had had little or nothing to say to anyone, and wished those days would return for a while. "Not now," he snapped. "Leave me alone, will you?"

Once again he hurried off, trying to lose Franklin in the crowd. For a moment he thought he'd done it—when he glanced behind him, there was no sign of the boy.

Then a second later, something hit him hard just behind the knees. There was no time to react; he felt his legs knocked out from under him.

"*Oof!*" He hit the ground with a thud. A second later, Franklin flung himself atop him, sitting upon his chest and glaring down into his face.

"You got to listen!" the boy exclaimed. "See here!" He reached into his grubby shirt and rummaged about.

Adam did his best to push him off, annoyed. "Why in blazes did you knock me down like that?" he cried. "Don't you see, if I don't figure out what to do, Ellie—"

"Here." Finally, Franklin found what he was looking for. He yanked out a folded letter and shoved it right in Adam's face.

Adam was ready to shove it back. But then the paper fell open, and Adam blinked. "Hey," he said. "Is that . . ."

Not bothering to go on, he struggled to sit up. This

time Franklin allowed him to do so, hopping off his chest and handing over the paper.

Adam stared at it, the truth dawning on him at last. There in his hand was the Brewsters' precious clue—the letter from President Jefferson to Meriwether Lewis that they believed would point them toward the treasure.

"Where did you get this?" he asked, still staring at the paper. As he'd deduced from the earlier glimpse, most of the words on it were pure gibberish. Only the first few lines were written in plain English, and they seemed bland enough to offer little in the way of a clue.

Franklin's eyes flashed with pride. "Reefed it," he said. "Right outta his pocket. Never saw me."

"You stole this from Stephen Brewster?" Adam couldn't help being impressed. The boy had guts. "But—why? Do you know what it is?"

Franklin stared at him somberly. "It's something important," he said. "Else they wouldn'ta stole it from the president's messenger. Knocked him over the head, they did." He touched his own grubby head as if in sympathy.

"So you witnessed that, did you?" It seemed Adam's earlier speculation had been correct. "That's why the

Brewsters held such a grudge against you, isn't it? They were afraid you'd tell someone what they'd done."

The boy shrugged. "Didn't know why," he mumbled. "Not till I heard him bragging to you about it on the coach. Me mum musta guessed though. Maybe it's why she wanted to leave Washington."

Adam realized that Franklin must have been feigning sleep while he and Miles were discussing the letter. Mingled feelings of awe, sympathy, and annoyance flooded through him.

But those feelings were soon displaced by another—hope. This letter was the bargaining chip he so desperately needed.

The Brewsters will probably do anything to get their clue back, he thought, his heart beating a little faster as the plan formed in his mind. *If I can catch up to them, I can offer to trade it back in exchange for Ellie's release.* He grimaced slightly. *Of course, this time I'll have to make certain they follow through. . . .*

He spared hardly a thought for his medallion, though he felt a twinge of regret as he recognized that indeed he was unlikely ever to see it again. But what matter was that when compared with the life of his sister?

"Come," he told Franklin with a swelling of nervous excitement. Tucking the letter into his pocket, he turned toward the river. "Let's see about hiring a boat. We're going to get Ellie back!"

Nine

Adam found it rather amazing that the same boatmen who had turned their backs on his pleas earlier suddenly became much more interested in his plight as soon as they realized he had money to pay for passage. Before long, he had his choice of at least half a dozen flatboats, skiffs, and pirogues.

He settled on a gruff, bristly bearded fur trader with a sturdy-looking scow that seemed able to make good time in the current with the assistance of its small mast and sail. The choice seemed even better when the trader named a figure that was less than one-third of the amount of money Adam had in his pocket.

"Done," Adam said at once, offering his hand to shake on the deal. Then he waved to Franklin, who was perched on a large coil of rope nearby. "Come on, let's go."

"Hold it!" The fur trader put out a hand to stop the boy from approaching the boat. "You didn't say nothing about *him.* That fare we just agreed on was for one passenger."

"But what difference does it make?" Adam argued. "I am hiring you for the journey, not by the passenger."

The man stroked his beard impassively. "If he comes along, he pays his fare."

For a moment, an annoyed Adam was ready to back out of their agreement and find a different boat. Perhaps one of the other boatmen would be willing to strike a better deal.

But then he realized that with every passing minute, Ellie and her captors were floating farther away down the river. Besides, few of the other vessels had sails, which seemed to greatly diminish their chances of catching the Brewsters' keelboat. For a moment he thought of leaving Franklin behind. But when he glanced at the boy's anxious face, he couldn't find it in him to do it. Odd as it might seem, Franklin appeared nearly as worried about Ellie's fate as Adam was himself.

"Fine," he said with a sigh, reaching for more money. "Here is his fare, then. Can we go? There is no time to lose."

"Aye. Off we go, then."

Soon the three of them were aboard the scow pushing out into the river. There was a small, roughly built shelter in the middle of the flat-bottomed boat, and Adam and Frank huddled there while the trader steered and adjusted the sail. For a while, both passengers were silent, lost in their own thoughts.

But then Franklin spoke up. "Think we'll catch her?" he asked, staring up at Adam with anxious eyes.

Adam shrugged, trying to look more confident than he felt. "Of course. And when we do, all we'll have to do is show them this." He pulled the letter out of his pocket.

If he hadn't been so worried about Ellie, it would have seemed a shame to give it up so easily. Partly out of curiosity and partly in hopes of distracting himself from his anxiety, he read over the text at the top of the page.

To Meriwether Lewis, Esq. Captain of the first regiment of infantry of the United States of America:

Pursuant to my earlier letters, I now offer you this confidential missive that I am trustful you alone shall be capable of deciphering to your great fortune. Thus, with preamble, I offer you these key words.

After that, the gibberish lines began. Adam squinted at them, wondering what they might mean.

"As I thought. It is most likely a simple substitution cipher," he said aloud.

"A what?"

Adam glanced up, realizing he'd nearly forgotten that Franklin was still present and listening. "A substitution cipher," he repeated. "My father and grandfather taught me all about such things. See, first one creates a *tabula recta*—that's a sort of square of alphabet letters, with each horizontal line shifting one spot to the left. So the first line begins with A and ends with Z, the second begins with B and ends with A, the third begins with C and ends with B, and so on. Do you see?"

He wondered belatedly if Franklin had any practical knowledge of the alphabet whatsoever. But the boy nodded as if he understood. "Then what?" he demanded.

"Then one chooses a keyword or line," Adam said, gripping the edge of the shelter as the scow bounced off a floating log and the boatman let out a curse. "It can be anything—say you decide that the key word would be your first name, Franklin, and the line you wished to encode was your surname, Poole. You would start with the first letter of each word, finding the *F* in Franklin in the top line of letters and the *P* in Poole in the vertical row going down the left side. Then you would follow each of those lines out to the spot within the *tabula recta* where they intersect. Whichever letter was found there would become the first letter of the coded line. In the case of our example, I believe that letter would be *U*. You would go on from there, doing each letter in turn. For example, the *R* in Franklin would be matched to the *O* in Poole, the *A* in Franklin would be matched to the second *O* and so forth. If the message you're trying to decode is longer than your keyword, you'd simply repeat the keyword from the beginning—in this case, the *F*. Anyone who wished to decode your message would need only be given the key word to do so, while anyone without that key would be unable to decipher it."

He wasn't sure he was explaining the substitution cipher clearly enough for his youthful and unschooled audience of one. But once again Franklin nodded, seeming to comprehend him well enough.

"So can you decipher it, then? The president's message to Mr. Clark?" Franklin glanced at the letter with new interest.

"As I just said, it is nearly impossible without knowing the keyword. And the keyword could be anything—probably some prearranged word or phrase decided on between the two of them at an earlier time."

"Oh." Franklin frowned. Then he turned away, looking disappointed.

Adam shrugged. As he returned the letter to his pocket, it got stuck for a moment on the corner of another paper within. Adam yanked out the second sheet, realizing it was the rough drawing of the medallion image.

"By the by, you never told me where you got this," he said, showing it to the boy.

Franklin pursed his lips. "Copied it down myself."

"But where did you see *this* image? On my medallion? Did you copy it from there?"

"Nope. Told you. Saw it out there." He waved one hand vaguely at the wooded shore.

Despite further questioning, that was all Franklin would say on the matter that day.

"**A**re you certain this lot are still ahead of us?" the boatman grumbled. "When I agreed to this job, I thought it would take me only a day or two downriver."

"That was not my understanding of our agreement, sir." Adam did his best to keep his voice and expression calm and nonconfrontational. "My intention is, and always has been, to catch up with my sister's captors."

Well over a week had passed on the river. As supplies dwindled, the fur trader's complaints had increased. Adam was beginning to fear that the man might insist on turning back or ending the journey at one of the settlements they passed now and then along the way. As it was, they'd been forced to pause for several hours at the village of Cincinnati to take on more food, which Adam had paid for out of his dwindling supply of money. He had chafed through every moment of the stop, imagining the Brewsters' keelboat drawing ever farther ahead.

"Well, we'd best catch up before the falls at Louisville," the boatman said with a frown.

Adam bit his lip, not sure how to respond. When he turned his head, he found Franklin staring at him with his unblinking dark eyes. The boy had barely said a word for the past three or four days. While Adam had never thought it possible, he found he missed the noise. Anything was better than the silence that engulfed him.

Later that day, however, Franklin let out an excited cry. "There they are!"

Adam scrambled for the front of the boat. Sure enough, another vessel was visible ahead, its sails billowing in the day's brisk wind.

"He's right!" he shouted. "That's the boat we want! Hurry, hurry!"

Grabbing an oar, he helped the fur trader push them faster ahead. Before long, they were close enough for those on the keelboat to take notice of them. Miles Brewster moved to the rear of his boat and shaded his eyes against the sun. When he saw who it was, he turned and shouted something over his shoulder.

"Where is my sister?" Adam called across the water.

A moment later, Stephen appeared beside his brother. "You!" he shouted, sounding displeased. "You followed us! You shall regret that, boy!"

"Where is my sister?" Adam cried again. "I have a deal to propose, but first I need to see that Ellie is safe."

The two brothers conferred for a moment, though the two boats were still many yards apart and Adam could not hear what they said. After a moment, Stephen cupped his hands and called out again: "What are you talking about?" he shouted. "What deal?"

"First I must see Ellie!"

Adam could see Stephen's mouth move in what was almost certainly an oath. But a moment later, Roger appeared from the keelboat's central cabin holding Ellie by the arm.

"Miss Ellie!" Franklin screamed.

Ellie let out a cry of her own. "Frank? Adam! Can it really be you?"

"It's us!" Despite the still grim situation, Adam broke into a broad grin at the sight and sound of his sister. "Are you all right?"

"I'm fine," she called back. "No thanks to these louts."

Adam chuckled. Being held captive by the Brewsters had done nothing to dampen his sister's spirits. If he knew her at all, he knew *she* had been the one to dampen theirs.

"You've seen her. Now what is this deal, Gates?" Stephen shouted.

Adam pulled the sheet of paper out of his pocket. "This," he called back, holding it up. "I have your precious letter from the president. If you return Ellie safely to me, I shall give it back to you."

Even at such a distance, he could see a look of surprise cross Stephen's face. But it lasted only a moment. Then Stephen let out a sharp laugh.

"Do you think us such fools, Gates?" he shouted. "Do you truly believe we would hold only one copy of that letter? No deal!"

Adam's heart sank. Before he could figure out what to do or say next, a shot rang out from the direction of the Brewsters' boat.

The fur trader swore loudly. "The devils are shooting at us!" he yelled, immediately steering hard to one side. "Blame it all, I didn't sign on for this sort of nonsense!"

Another shot came, and Adam flung himself to the rough bottom of the scow. "Get down, Frank!" he called.

He could hear Ellie screaming at the Brewsters to stop, though it was hard to make out her every word over the continued sound of the fur trader's oaths. After another shot, there was silence from ahead. Lifting his head cautiously, Adam saw that the keelboat was by now quite some distance ahead and pulling away rapidly.

"That's it," the fur trader said. "This trip is over."

"No!" Adam sat up quickly. "Please. We have to keep after them."

His heart was still pounding from the close call. But he couldn't give up. There had to be a way to rescue Ellie.

It took only a few minutes for Adam to bribe the boatman into continuing by giving him the rest of his money. However, it took the rest of the afternoon and some help from Franklin to figure out a new way to help Ellie. But by nightfall, they had settled on a plan.

First, while the sun was fading from the sky, they drew just near enough to the Brewsters' keelboat to keep it in view without being noticed themselves. They waited until it was fully dark, then extinguished their lantern and drew even closer.

"All right," Adam whispered to Franklin, keeping his mouth as close as possible to the boy's ear to avoid his voice carrying over the water. "Do you know what to do?"

"Yes," the boy hissed back. "Are you certain Miss Ellie can swim?"

"Well enough," Adam replied. "But that is why we both must go to help her."

He felt, rather than saw, the boy nod in the dark. Then he crept over to the fur trader.

"We shall return shortly," he whispered to the man. "When you hear us swimming back, light the lantern so that we shall know where to aim. Be prepared to extinguish it once we're aboard in case they try to shoot at us again."

The man sighed. "As you wish," he grumbled. While handsomely paid, it made him no more pleased to be taking part in the plan.

But Adam couldn't pause to worry about that. Touching Franklin on the shoulder, he stepped to the edge of the scow and lowered himself into the river. A moment later, Franklin slipped off the boat as well.

The cold water made Adam gasp with shock, and the current was stronger than he'd expected, even though the boatman had assured them that this spot would be calmer than most. Kicking out as strongly as he could, he headed toward the single light flickering aboard the Brewsters' boat. He hoped he hadn't asked too much of young Franklin by bringing him along. What if the river overcame him?

But he did his best not to think about that. Instead, he focused on the task at hand. It seemed to take forever to reach the keelboat. But when he finally put his hand out and touched its rough wooden side, he found that Franklin was right beside him.

They didn't need to speak, having already planned out what came next. Franklin scrambled up onto the keelboat with Adam's assistance and crept off toward the central cabin. Meanwhile, Adam bobbed in the cold water, hanging on to the side of the boat and doing his best to catch his breath for the return swim. As ten seconds ticked by and then twenty, he itched to know what was happening and almost gave into the urge to hoist himself aboard. But he managed to hold back. He had already figured out that the small, lightweight Franklin would be less likely to awaken the Brewsters or attract notice if one of them was on guard. He would just have to trust his instinct.

A moment later, he heard the soft scuffle of footsteps very close by. He held his breath, ready to duck underwater should a Brewster appear.

Instead, he heard a soft female whisper: "Damad?"

"Lee-ell!" he whispered back in relief. "Ree-hurr. Start mingswim wardtow our boatflat. Franklin and I will sistass you if you come-be erd-tire."

"Stoodderun, therbro," Ellie murmured.

Adam felt a swelling of pride. How many young ladies would react so calmly and sensibly to such a situation?

"Hey!" a rough voice shouted, shattering the silence of the night. "Where's that girl at?"

"Go!" Adam shouted, knowing that there was little sense in being quiet any longer. They had been caught in the act. Even so, they had the advantage of surprise and the cover of darkness on their side. They could still make it.

Ellie leaped into the river with a splash. By now, the other two Brewsters were awake and shouting as well. In the confusion, Adam managed to find his sister in the water and grasp her arm.

"This way," he whispered, hoping that his sense of direction was good. It was difficult to gauge much of anything in the dark. "Come on. When we're close enough, our boatman will light a candle to show us the way."

They swam away from the keelboat. Franklin found them after a moment as well, paddling swiftly on Ellie's other side. Adam could hear his sister gasping for breath.

"Oh, it is so c-c-c-cold!" she chattered.

"Don't talk," Adam advised her, his own breath coming

in short spurts. "Save energy for swimming."

A shot rang out over their heads. Ellie let out a yelp.

"Hush!" Franklin hissed urgently. "They cannot see us. Don't let them hear nothing neither."

It was good advice and Ellie obeyed instantly, not saying another word. Adam did his best not to splash too much as he swam, and he could tell the others were doing the same.

Finally, he gauged that they had to be coming close to where the scow should be. He let out a whistle, as pre-arranged with the boatman. They all paused, treading water and waiting for the return light to flare.

But a full minute passed, and the only light came from the keelboat, where several lanterns were now glowing. Judging by the sounds from that direction, the Brewsters had turned and were rowing after them.

His heart pounding, Adam whistled again, more loudly this time. When there was still no response, he called out the boatman's name.

"It's no good," Franklin whispered hoarsely. "He's run off!"

"No! He wouldn't dare!" Refusing to believe it, Adam let out another loud whistle.

"This way, boys!" Stephen's voice rang out. "I hear 'em!"

"It's no use, Adam!" Ellie whispered urgently. "Your boat's gone, or we went the wrong way. In either case, we can't stay here or they'll soon find us—if we don't freeze to death in the meantime. Swim for shore!"

Adam knew she was right. His heart sank as he recognized the certain truth—the fur trader had seen his chance to extricate himself from this inconvenient mission, and he'd taken it—never mind that he knew he was leaving them to certain peril. With a soft oath, he struck out for shore beside the others.

It seemed almost a miracle when his feet struck ground some minutes later, just as it felt his lungs might give out. Even more miraculously, as he staggered through the rocky shallows onto dry ground, Ellie was beside him clutching his hand, and he could hear Franklin nearby. The moon was rising by now, and he could make out their weary forms struggling up the riverbank.

But the miracles ended there. "There they are just ahead!" Miles yelled from an alarmingly close locale. "I see them! They've just gone ashore—just there! Let's be after them, boys!"

Ten

With a groan, Adam realized that the danger was only beginning. "Run!" he called to Ellie and Frank. "Quickly! We must try to lose them in the woods."

They plunged into the thick forest at the top of the riverbank. Almost immediately, any light from the moon was extinguished by the thick canopy of branches, vines, and emerging spring leaves overhead. Adam's face was scratched by a million unseen twigs, and vines seemed to reach out to trip him up with every step. He kept a tight grip on Ellie's hand and pushed on, not knowing what else to do.

A moment later, he heard the scraping of the keelboat in the shallows and then heavy, running footsteps. A glance back showed a lantern bobbing through the trees just a dozen yards behind. For a second, Adam felt all the energy leave his body. What was the use? Even if they could outpace their pursuers, which seemed unlikely, they would then be lost in the untamed wilderness, miles from civilization and safety. They might as well give up and throw themselves on the Brewsters' mercy.

"This way—follow me!" Franklin hissed. "Come on, come on!"

"Come, Adam." Ellie gave a tug on his hand. "We must follow Frank. Hurry!"

Without much hope, but not knowing what else to do, Adam obeyed. The boy led them on a sharp turn to the left, moving faster than before. For a minute or two, the way continued to be difficult to navigate, with fierce snarls of vines and thick, prickly underbrush. But then Adam felt the vines thin out and a beaten dirt path open beneath his soggy shoes. Could it be? Somehow, Franklin had found a trail.

They were able to make much better time then, breaking into a full-out run along the narrow, twisting path through the trees, a track that had almost certainly been made by wild animals. The sounds of the Brewsters cursing and breaking branches soon fell behind.

"Over here," Franklin hissed. This time he angled off to the right on another, even narrower track. A moment later, he paused. "A cave! We can hide in here, all right?"

Sure enough, in the faint moonlight filtering through the treetops, Adam saw a dark opening in a cluster of rocks. It appeared just large enough for the three of them to squeeze into.

As they huddled in the mouth of the cave, doing their best to keep their panting as quiet as possible, Adam found himself amazed by how agile and comfortable Franklin seemed in the thick, wild forest. Then again, he supposed it shouldn't have been a surprise. He and Ellie had already deduced that the boy must have spent much of his time since arriving in Pittsburgh out exploring—and maybe even living in—the wilderness. It seemed that their assumption had been correct, and more importantly, that Franklin's exploration had paid off.

They sat a long time in silence. Finally deciding the Brewsters hadn't followed them, they crawled out of the cave and Franklin led the way back to the riverbank. Peering out, they saw that the moon was directly overhead by now, casting a silvery pallor over the broad river.

"Look," Ellie whispered, pointing downstream. "There they go."

Adam followed her gaze and saw the keelboat drifting

along with the current. For a moment he felt relief. The brothers had given up the chase.

But then a wild, eerie howl rang out from somewhere in the dense forest surrounding them, and that relief was instantly replaced with dread. True, they had rescued Ellie from the Brewsters and escaped their pursuit. But now what? They were a very long way from Pittsburgh—or anything else resembling real civilization—with no boat, no supplies, and no idea which way to go to find the closest settlement.

Still, he didn't want to frighten Ellie or Franklin with such ideas. So he carefully kept his voice calm and cheerful as he spoke. "Come," he said. "Let's return to that cave, shall we? We can rest there until morning and decide then how to proceed."

By the time the sun rose, Adam was already awake. He had fallen asleep almost immediately upon lying down in the cave, exhausted not only from the night's adventure but also from many long days of worry. But his anxiety hadn't allowed him to rest for long.

Ellie and Franklin soon awoke, as well. There was a freshwater stream nearby, allowing them to drink and wash.

Then, Franklin set about collecting a variety of roots, leaves, and nuts for their breakfast. Once again, Adam couldn't help being impressed as he watched the boy. How had he picked up so much knowledge on his own? It showed a curious and resourceful mind, indeed.

"Here, what about this?" he called out to Franklin, leaning down to pluck a few small, tender-looking branch shoots from a soft needle-leaved shrub. "Looks rather tasty."

Ellie and Franklin both wandered over. "Nice find, Adam," Ellie said. "Perhaps we'll make an outdoorsman of you yet!"

Adam chuckled. "Perhaps." Glancing at Franklin, he added, "Would you like some?"

Franklin shook his head wordlessly. He held up his own handful of gathered food.

"Suit yourself." Adam shrugged. "Ellie? What about you?"

"Thanks." Ellie accepted one of the branch tips Adam had picked. "I hope this tastes better than that root I just ate."

"Wait, Miss Ellie," Franklin blurted out. "Don't eat that."

"What?" Adam had just tossed the first shoot into his mouth, though he hadn't started to chew. "Why shouldn't she eat it?"

The boy shrugged. "Deadly poison."

His eyes widening, Adam spat out the shoot. "What?" He wiped his mouth on his sleeve, then stuck out his tongue and wiped that, too. "Why didn't you say so? I was about to eat that!"

"I *did* say so." Frank stared at him, as if daring him to argue. "Just now."

Adam frowned. He and the boy had been getting along well enough during their journey down the river, at least as compared to before. But apparently, that didn't mean they were friends.

Still, he decided not to fuss about it. No harm done, after all. Besides, all he had to do was get them all back to civilization, and then he could rid himself of the boy for good.

"All right," he said, tossing the rest of the shoots he'd picked into the underbrush. "Now that we've had some breakfast, let's decide what to do next. I've been thinking about it, and I think we should head back to the river and flag down the next boat that passes in either direction. If we're lucky, we might get one going upriver and catch a ride back to Pittsburgh. Even if we end up going the other way, that fur trader kept grumbling about Louisville being not terribly far downriver. We should be able to arrange transport back east from there, or from any other settlement of decent size."

"Then again, perhaps we should continue all the way downriver to St. Louis," Ellie put in eagerly. "If Lewis and Clark haven't departed their winter camp yet, we might yet be able to convince them to take us along!"

Franklin looked intrigued by the suggestion. For a moment, Adam shared the feeling. His hand wandered toward the pocket where he held the medallion drawing and the president's letter. What if . . .

But then he shook his head, banishing such thoughts. This was certainly not the time to allow his impulsive side to take over. No, the time for adventure and spontaneity was over. This was a time to act more as George might. Responsibly. Taking care of Ellie and Franklin, keeping them safe, getting them back to civilization.

"No," he said firmly. "As soon as we reach a settlement,

we shall send for money from home and then take the first coach back to the coast."

Ellie frowned. "But what is the point of that?" she cried. "Perhaps it is providence that has brought us this far and is pointing us onward toward even greater adventure."

"Yeah," Franklin put in. "Could be."

Adam shook his head. "This is for the best," he said. "Besides, chances are by the time we could reach St. Louis, the expedition will be gone. According to the talk around Pittsburgh, Lewis and Clark intended to set out as soon as the weather allowed."

"Perhaps." Ellie stared at him. "But that doesn't mean we shouldn't try. We could even catch up to them if they hadn't gone far yet. After all, they intend to follow the river upstream—it wouldn't be difficult to hire a boat and—"

"Hire a boat? With what money?" Adam cut her off. He shook his head. "No, it is decided. This adventure ends as soon as we can arrange our journey home."

"But—" Franklin began.

"Never mind, Frank," Ellie interrupted, shooting Adam a sour glance. "Apparently, my bossy brother has decided that he is an American King George all of a sudden. What point is there in arguing with such a pronouncement?"

"Ellie . . ." Adam began.

But she had already turned away, taking Franklin by the hand as she did. "Come," she said. "Let's head back to the river as our master orders."

"Lee-ell," Adam said coaxingly. "Tenlis to me. Linfrank is ree-ver young, and it is usgerdange here in the nessderwill. . . ."

"Stop that!" Franklin shot him an irritated look over his shoulder. "I know you're talking in code."

"He is saying nothing of importance, Frank." Ellie tugged him onward. "Come, let us watch for interesting birds in the trees as we walk, shall we?"

She paid no further mind to Adam, marching on ahead hand in hand with the boy. Adam sighed, feeling bad about his own clumsy attempt at leadership as he trailed after them. But what else could he do? It was clear that neither of the other two had any sense whatsoever. That left their safety entirely up to him, and he wasn't going to let them down—whether they liked it or not.

"See? It works like this. You go along the top line here until you reach the letter *F* for Frank." Ellie pointed with the stick she'd used to sketch out a *tabula recta* in the soft mud of the river's edge. "Then you go down the letters on the side here until you find the first letter of your keyword. . . ."

Adam glanced over from where he was seated on a large rock farther along the riverbank. A couple of days had passed since that first night in the forest. After waiting a few hours on the riverbank where they'd landed, Adam had decided that they might as well start walking downstream beside the river. He figured there was a better chance of catching a boat heading south than north, especially this time of year, and there was no point in sitting around when they could be moving—especially if the Brewsters should decide to return and search for them.

So far not a single boat had passed, at least not during daylight hours. Still, Adam was sure one would be along soon enough. He was already looking forward to the comforts of civilization, including a hot meal, a soft bed, and the company of people who weren't holding a grudge against him.

But for the moment, as they rested and ate more of the nuts and roots that Franklin had procured for them, Adam couldn't help listening as Ellie repeated the lesson he'd already given the boy on ciphers. She wasn't *trying* to keep him from hearing—though she and Franklin pointedly excluded him from most of their conversations.

"See there?" Ellie pointed to whatever she'd just written with her stick. "That's how you would translate your name into code. To decipher it, one would only have to reverse the process. If we could guess the keyword or phrase, we would surely have little trouble deciphering that letter you took from the Brewsters. What do you think Mr. Jefferson might have chosen?"

Franklin looked thoughtful. "D'you think those bad men will figure it out? Or the medallion, either?"

Ellie shrugged. "I doubt it." She scribbled idly in the mud with her stick. "But the more important question is why do you suppose they wanted that old medallion? It can't possibly have anything to do with the treasure they're seeking, or anything else in this part of the world."

"But I saw it," Franklin said. He shot a look at Adam. "Didn't he tell you? Out here." He waved a hand at their sur-roundings.

"What do you mean?" Ellie shot her brother a brief look before returning her gaze to the boy. "Adam mentioned that you'd sketched out the medallion's markings, but he seemed to think you must have seen it in the coach when he was showing it to Miles."

"No! I told him!" Franklin shook his head. "I saw it. *Not* on his blasted medallion. I copied it off a rock in the woods. Near the city."

"Really? Near Pittsburgh?" Ellie sounded confused. "But what could that marking have been doing out there? The medallion comes from Roanoke. Or perhaps Jamestown. Either way, that's a long way from here."

Adam was wondering the same thing. All this time, he realized, Franklin had been telling him that he'd seen the marking out in the wilderness. Somehow, though, he hadn't really heard it until now. He felt a spark of curiosity flare up inside him—a spark that had been dampened since taking control of this trip. How *had* that symbol come to be carved on a rock in the remote wilderness outside of Pittsburgh?

Maybe the Brewsters have the right idea, after all, he thought. *If Lewis and Clark really are after some immense treasure—perhaps even the Treasure of the Ancients!—that coded letter is probably their guide. And what if my lie wasn't really a lie and my medallion holds some clue as well? True, our family lore holds that the medallion comes from an old native woman near Jamestown and involves a treasure from Roanoke. But who is to say that's true? Nobody alive really knows for sure. Besides, the Treasure of the Ancients is rumored to have been on this continent nearly as far back as the time of the Lost Colony of Roanoke, according to Grandfather's old stories. . . .*

His heart started beating a little faster as he thought of the possibilities. For a moment he was ready to give in and do as his sister and Franklin wanted. Perhaps it wasn't such a crazy notion, after all. They could find their way to St. Louis, meet up with Lewis and Clark and convince them somehow to take them all along. . . .

But just then a flash of movement caught his eye from the direction of the river. He looked up, expecting to see a flock of birds or some other such sight. Instead, he saw a boat making its laborious way upriver by means of a pair of men poling and rowing.

The welcome sight sent everything else flying out of Adam's head at once.

"Hey!" he shouted, leaping to his feet and waving his arms over his head. "Over here! Help us, please!"

Ellie and Franklin looked up from their code-making. When she saw the vessel, Ellie let out a gasp. "Oh," she said. "It seems we are rescued at last."

Adam was still jumping up and down. He'd ripped off his jacket and was waving it over his head like a flag, not wanting the boat to miss them.

"Here!" he cried eagerly. "We are stranded, and we need to . . ." The words trailed off as the men on the boat looked toward him and let out an answering shout. A third man appeared from the cabin in the center. Adam gasped as the boat drew close enough for him to make out their faces.

"Blazes," Franklin exclaimed at that moment. "It's them!"

Adam couldn't believe their bad luck. It was the Brewsters and their keelboat! And they were already poling straight toward them.

"Quick," Adam exclaimed. "Back into the woods—run!"

Behind him, he heard a splash as the Brewsters leaped into the shallows. "We've got them this time, boys," Stephen's all-too-familiar voice roared.

"This way." Franklin passed Adam as they entered the woods.

This time Adam didn't hesitate, following as the boy raced nimbly along a barely perceptible trail, effortlessly dodging brambles and leaping over exposed roots. Ellie was close behind him, panting with fear and exertion.

"We lost them once," Adam called back to her, not wanting her to lose heart. "We can do it again."

But this time the Brewsters had daylight on their side, and they didn't seem inclined to give up nearly so easily as they had before. Franklin led them down one forest path and up another, over lumpy hills covered with rocks and through swamps and sunny clearings. But this time they couldn't seem to lose the Brewsters. Every time they thought they'd pulled ahead, there would come a shout as the men spotted them through the trees or scrambling over one of the many rocky outcroppings that seemed to inhabit this section of the forest.

An hour passed, and Adam could tell that Ellie wouldn't be able to go on much longer. He wasn't sure how much longer he could continue himself. They had to be miles from the river by now; the sun was directly overhead, and he'd lost all sense of direction. Their escape was beginning to seem hopeless; no matter how far they went, there was nothing to stop the Brewsters from tracking them.

"We need to find a place to stop," he panted, catching

up to Franklin, who was still in the lead. "We need to rest and think of a plan."

"We can't," the boy said. "They're still coming."

Adam glanced back at Ellie. Her cheeks were pink, and her brow dotted with perspiration. "Look, we just passed a big outcropping back there on the left," he said. "Let's double back and make a run for it. They won't be expecting us to try something like that. Plus, we won't leave prints on the rock if we climb up into it. Perhaps we can find a spot to hide behind a boulder or something and let them go by."

"Won't work," Franklin said.

But Adam knew there was no time to argue over it. If they wanted to double back, they had to do it now before the Brewsters got close enough to spot them.

"Come on," he cried, grabbing Ellie by the arm. "Back this way!"

"Wait!" Franklin exclaimed.

Adam ignored him. Racing along the path they'd just traveled, he veered off after a few dozen yards, heading to the right. He'd seen the tip of some sort of rocky bluff over the trees over that way, one of the largest so far.

When they emerged from the tree line, they found themselves in a large, open area at the base of the bluff, which was even more enormous than Adam had guessed—it was some thirty feet high and stretched from left to right as far as the eye could see. Adam's heart sank. There was no rocky scree or hard ground immediately before them. Instead, they found themselves at the edge of a damp, low-lying area surrounding a meandering stream. There was a broad, dry, grassy meadow beyond, which sloped gently upward toward the base of the bluff. But to get there required first crossing the swampy field, which would show their prints as clearly as could be.

"Never mind," Adam cried. "This won't work. We've got to get back and keep—"

"There they are! I see them!"

Ellie let out a cry of fear at the sound of Miles's voice behind them. "They've found us!"

"Come on." It was too late to double back again. Adam grabbed Ellie's hand and raced forward. "We have to keep going. There's no other way."

They crossed the swampy area, jumping the stream, and then continued across the dry meadow with the tall grasses whispering against their legs. Soon they were at the base of the bluff. Adam had been hoping that somehow they'd be able to scale the rocky ridge. But he quickly realized that was a hopeless plan. For one thing, it was far too steep. More importantly, it soon became evident that the Brewsters had not come without their firearms. A shot rang out, causing Adam and the others to dart behind a large boulder near the base of the cliff.

"Let's just keep going." Adam tried not to sound as desperate as he felt, though he suspected that it would be impossible to be any more panicked at this moment. "Keep behind the larger boulders as much as possible. This bluff must end sooner or later, and then we can go around."

But the bluff seemed to go on forever. Adam expected the Brewsters to catch up to them at any moment. Instead, he heard them calling to one another out in the meadow. What were they doing? Was this their cruel way of enjoying the last few moments of their cat-and-mouse game?

Ellie seemed to be wondering the same thing. "Why don't they just end this?" she cried, sounding exhausted. "They must know they have us."

"I don't know." Adam drew in a breath, then coughed.

He sniffed the air, realizing the scent of smoke had appeared.

Peering out around the edge of the boulder behind which they were currently sheltering, his eyes widened. Flames were flickering among the dry meadow grasses beyond the bluff. For a second he stared, not understanding where the fire had come from. But then he realized what it had to mean. The Brewsters must have set that fire. They intended to burn them out of hiding!

Eleven

The smoke was soon so thick that all of them started coughing. "It's no use!" Ellie cried. "We'll have to give up, or choke to death. Why are they so determined to capture us, anyway?"

Adam suspected he knew the answer. Surely, the Brewsters had realized that he was now in possession of both clues—firstly, the president's coded letter; and secondly, the medallion, which may or may not have something to do with the letter. That made him doubly dangerous to their quest. And of course, there was young Franklin as well—surely they hadn't forgiven or forgotten that he'd witnessed their crime against Jefferson's messenger back in Washington's city. . . .

But there was no time to explain any of that. "Keep going," Adam urged instead, putting an arm around Ellie to help her along as they dashed for the shelter of the next boulder, coughing all the while.

However, the situation seemed impossible. The bluff continued on, still rising overhead in a rock wall too sheer to scale. The fire blocked their escape back to the woods, with the Brewsters lurking somewhere on the other side with their muskets. For a second, Adam was ready to admit that Ellie was right—they might as well give up. There was no way out.

Then Ellie let out a cry. "There!" she cried, pointing through the hazy, smoky air toward the rock wall just ahead. "Is that—can it be an opening? Perhaps we can . . ."

Her voice trailed off in a fit of coughing, but it didn't matter. Both Adam and Franklin had instantly understood the implication.

"Come on," Adam cried. "It's a cave! We have to try it—there's no other hope."

They dashed ahead and ducked in through the narrow opening in the rock. The cave opened up inside, though it was too dark to see how deep it went into the bluff. Adam knew that if it turned out to be a dead end, it would likely be a true *dead* end for the three of them.

"Ow!" Adam blurted out as his toe struck a rough spot in the floor, sending him crashing into the hard rock wall.

"Hush!" Franklin hissed from the darkness.

Adam blinked, trying to see anything at all. The scant light from the entrance had faded fast. "Where are you two?" he whispered hoarsely, feeling a flutter of panic.

"I'm here," Ellie whispered, her voice reassuring. "Adam? Walk toward my voice. Frank is here with me already."

"Keep talking." Adam stuck both hands out before him, not wanting to crash into another hard wall. Ellie softly hummed a tune, and he followed the sound until he sensed her hands grappling toward him.

"There," she said, gripping his hand tightly in her own. "Now, this cave seems to be sloping downward."

Adam realized she was right. He hadn't been fully aware of it, but now that he paid it some mind, he could feel the ground dropping downward as they moved farther from the cave's entrance.

"That's fine," he whispered back. "But what shall we do if it ends? Do you think if we hide and keep very quiet—"

"It won't end," Franklin pointed out.

"He's correct, Adam," Ellie whispered. "Can you not feel the cool air coming toward us? It would not be doing that were we not entering a passage underground. With any luck, it will carry us beneath the bluff and out the other side, where perhaps we shall finally be able to lose our pursuers."

Adam felt a bit foolish. He hadn't even noticed the cold breeze wafting toward them from deeper underground.

I suppose that's because I do not share Ellie's great knowledge of the natural world, he admitted to himself. *Nor even young Frank's strange comfort in it. All this time I have been endeavoring to lead them to safety, but perhaps they should have been leading me.*

Another worry occurred to him. "How shall we find our way with no light?" he murmured even as Ellie tugged him along a few steps deeper into the passage.

"Frank has his free hand on the wall," Ellie replied calmly. "All we need do is follow it until we come out the other end. Now, we probably shouldn't speak until we are certain the Brewsters haven't followed us in here, all right?"

"Yes, good idea." Adam clutched his sister's hand and shuffled along behind her. It felt rather eerie to be moving along with no visual sense of where he was. In fact, he had trouble knowing from one moment to the next whether his eyes were open or closed. He tried not to imagine how at every step they might go plunging into a bottomless pit or walk straight into the jaws of some fearsome underground beast.

Instead, he focused on holding on to Ellie's hand and putting one foot in front of the other. The going was slow but steady. Franklin would occasionally warn them in a whisper of an obstacle in the path or a curve in one direction or other. Otherwise, they didn't speak. The downward slope of the tunnel continued, causing Adam to wonder exactly how deep below the ground they were by now.

With no sun to see, it was difficult to keep track of the hour; by the time Franklin spoke to warn them of a fork in the tunnel, Adam had no idea how many minutes had passed since they'd left the blazing meadow.

"Which way shall we go?" Ellie whispered. Then she cleared her throat and spoke in her normal voice. "Er, I think it's safe to talk aloud by now. I don't think they've followed us down here. We would have heard them."

There came the sound of shuffling as Franklin moved ahead. "The left fork keeps going down," he announced after a moment. "The other way stays level."

"I expect the level way is the better choice then, is it not?" Adam said.

"Yes," Franklin agreed. "Come along, let's keep going. I'll stay in the lead—I'm checking with my foot for holes in the floor so you won't fall, Miss Ellie."

At the boy's earnest words, Adam was glad that the others couldn't see his flush of shame in the darkness. All along, he'd been allowing a child to risk his life leading them to safety. Had the dark tunnel robbed him of all sense of courage, let alone adventurous spirit?

"No, let me lead the way," he said quickly, pushing past Ellie and in the process scraping his elbow on the opposite wall, which was closer than he'd realized.

"You don't know nothing about caves," Franklin argued. "You're liable to lead us all into a hole or some such."

"Why don't you take turns?" Ellie spoke up soothingly. "It is too exhausting for either of you to be on alert the entire time. Franklin, let Adam lead for now while you take a break. He will be careful, I am certain. Then you can switch back in a little while."

"Very well." Franklin's tone was grudging. "If *you* say so, Miss Ellie."

"Fine. Let's switch, then."

Adam fumbled his way forward, telling himself it was

surely an accident when Franklin's small foot came down hard on his own as he passed in the darkness. Soon they were situated in the opposite order from before. Adam was holding Ellie's hand with his own right hand. Putting his left hand against the cool, rough, slightly damp stone of the tunnel wall, he shivered, partly from the chilly air and partly out of nervousness at stepping forward into the total unknown. But he took a deep breath and forced himself onward. With each step, he felt about with his toes to be sure the floor was still there as solid as ever.

After a few minutes, his toe caught on a loose bit of rock and he stumbled slightly before recovering. Ellie let out a gasp and gripped his hand more tightly than ever.

"What was that?" she asked, the slight edge in her voice betraying fear. "Are you all right, Adam?"

"Yes. I'm fine."

For the first time since entering the cave, Adam forgot his own fears. His sister had to be just as terrified as he was himself, even if she'd been hiding it well until then. Furthermore, it was impossible to imagine that a child of Franklin's age was not anxious as well, even if he wasn't showing it. Adam might not have the same wilderness skills as the others, but he realized there was one area in which he was well qualified to help. He could distract them from their fears and make them think of other, more pleasant matters than this dank, dark cave in which they were creeping along.

"Listen, you two," he said in a voice as cheerful as he could manage, "it's awfully dull walking along like this with nothing to look at, isn't it? Why don't we try to divert ourselves a bit? I heard an amusing joke back in Pittsburgh involving a simpleminded man from the countryside and a Philadelphia lawyer. . . ."

For the next little while, he kept up a steady stream of chatter. First, he got Ellie chuckling with some silly jokes and riddles—and once or twice, he thought he heard a soft snort of laughter from Franklin, as well. When he ran out of jokes, he switched over to challenging them with word puzzles and bits of code. While this was a regular pastime for himself and Ellie, Franklin caught on quickly and soon was nearly as clever with his answers as Ellie herself.

"You have a nimble mind indeed, Frank," Adam said admiringly. He immediately winced in anticipation of the boy's sharp retort. But, instead, there was a moment of silence before Franklin spoke.

"Me mum said I got that from me dad," the boy said at last, his voice soft and uncertain. "He was always clever with his mind as well as his hands."

"What happened to your father, Franklin?" Ellie asked gently.

There was another moment of silence and Adam began to think the boy didn't mean to answer. Then Franklin spoke again.

"He brought us over from Ireland because he heard there was lots of work here," he said. "Sure enough, he got him a job right off. He helped build the presidential mansion in the new capital city."

The design and building of the impressive white presidential palace in Washington had been in the news since Adam was a boy. He had heard of the many Irish, Scottish, and Italian immigrants who had helped erect it. President Adams had moved in some three and a half years ago, soon followed by President Jefferson when he took over the office.

"Imagine it! Building the house where the United States

president would live," Adam said. "That must have been a rip-roaring job."

"Not for me dad. Got killed by a falling bit of stone just before it was finished." The boy's voice hardened. "That left me and mum on our own, with no family or friends about. Mum spent the last three, four years begging for what we could get, and me, too, soon's I was old enough. S'what we was doing when I saw them Brewsters knock down the president's messenger and steal the letter."

"Blazes," Adam exclaimed softly with a rush of true sympathy. All along he'd thought of Franklin Poole as little more than an irritant, an extra problem to be managed among many others. But hearing of the hardships he'd been through already in his short life—not to mention recalling all the help he'd been on this journey, from leading Adam to the docks in search of Ellie to finding their way safely through this cave—made Adam wonder if he hadn't been too quick to ignore the boy's good qualities only because of his scowl and sharp tongue.

Such thoughts gave rise to a new resolve. If the three of them escaped from this latest adventure alive and returned safely to civilization, he wouldn't abandon Franklin back onto the streets all alone. Such an idea was now unthinkable. Perhaps the Gates family could become the family Franklin now lacked. Surely, they could find a job for him at the stables or harness shop back home so he could put that clever mind of his to better use than begging on the street.

"Well," Ellie said after another moment of silence. "Is it time to let Frank take another turn in the lead? Or perhaps you'd like me to take a shift?"

"No, Miss Ellie," Franklin said immediately. "I'll do it."

They made the switch. "All right," Ellie said cheerfully. "Who has another code to challenge us?"

Adam smiled to himself in the dark, realizing she was changing the subject for the sake of the boy. "Hmm, let me think . . ." he began.

"What about that letter?" Franklin spoke up. "Shouldn't we be trying to guess that keyword so's we can solve the clue?"

"Oh, Frank." Ellie clucked softly. "That key could be anything! Any word, any phrase, a name, even a poem . . . Why, one would need to be able to read the president's mind to guess it."

"I'm not so sure about that," Adam said, not wanting to

quash the boy's interest. "It has to be something he and Lewis both would know and remember. Perhaps a word such as 'expedition' or 'Freemason' . . ."

"Or 'treasure'!" Franklin suggested eagerly.

"All right, then. What about 'Louisiana'?" Ellie put in.

They spent the next few minutes tossing out more ideas. But eventually they all seemed to realize that there was little more they could do on the matter until they could sketch out a *tabula recta* and test some of the keys. That would have to wait until they found their way out of the dark cave. So talk turned next to that medallion symbol.

"Where exactly did you see it, Frank?" Adam asked.

"Out in the woods to the west—other side of the river." For the first time, the boy's answer was matter-of-fact, with no trace of hostility. "Saw it first on a rock. The arrow on the side was pointing to the northwest, so I went that way."

"Hang on a moment." Adam was startled. "Did you say you saw it *first* on a rock? Was there a second mark elsewhere?"

"That's what I'm telling you." Franklin sounded a bit impatient again. "Went to the northwest a ways, then saw the same picture carved on a big old tree. Least I think it was the same. Harder to see, 'cause it was grown into the bark some. Anyway, this time it pointed straight west."

"Did you follow the arrow to the west?" Ellie sounded curious.

"Started to," Franklin replied. "Got chased by a bear and had to turn back. Didn't have a chance to try again before I ran into you two again."

"Blazes," Adam murmured. "So the medallion *is* a clue! Or, at the very least, a map!"

He could hardly believe it. After spending his entire life hearing all the tales and legends connected with the old family heirloom, he thought of it in much the same light as other sorts of tales he'd been told as a child. But now, thanks to Franklin, the medallion's history seemed much more real than that. It really could be leading to a treasure left by the long-lost settlers from Roanoke! Or perhaps even be connected somehow to the Treasure of the Ancients, as the Brewsters seemed to assume.

"All right, but even if the arrow makes sense now, what about the rest of the symbol?" he mused aloud. "That human-looking figure in the middle, with the six slashes through it . . . it must have some meaning. . . ."

Discussing that kept the three of them occupied for another hour or more. Adam was just beginning to wonder if they would be wandering around underground forever, when he realized he could now see Ellie as a vague, grayish shape before him. He gasped.

"Look!" he cried. "There, ahead—it's getting lighter. We must be reaching the other end!"

"Sakes alive!" Ellie exclaimed. "I was starting to fear we'd never see sunlight again."

They hurried forward, no longer caring if they stumbled over loose rocks in the path. Adam's heart thumped with anticipation. With any luck the long journey underground meant they'd lost the Brewsters for good. All they had to do now was return to the riverbank, follow it upstream or down, and await another passing boat that could carry them to Pittsburgh or Louisville or some other settlement where a coach could be found.

Adam's footsteps grew quicker as the light grew stronger. Before long, he was running full out, the others at his heels. He burst out into the open air, grinning with joy to see the sun in the sky, though by this time it was very low over the horizon.

"We made it!" he exclaimed, spinning around to get his bearings.

His smile faded. Nothing around him looked familiar. The composition of the trees in the forest looked very different than that of the forest they'd left on the other end of the cave. The color of the rocks was nothing like that of the bluff where they'd entered. And even when they climbed the highest hill around to get a better look, the river was nowhere to be seen in any direction. It seemed they were well and truly lost.

Twelve

Adam stared hopelessly toward the horizon, his eyes glancing in every direction. With the sun so low in the sky, he knew that any large body of water would throw off a reflection that would allow it to be seen for miles.

"We must have walked even farther than I thought down there," he murmured.

In one sense, that was a good thing. There was no way the Brewsters would ever be able to find them now. On the other hand, it meant they were lost themselves.

"It is all right, Mr. Adam," Franklin said, "I can lead us back to the river."

"You can?" Adam stared at him, so startled by his assurance that he barely noticed that, for the first time in memory, the boy had addressed him by his proper name.

Franklin shrugged. "I can tell where we are by the place of the sun in the sky," he said confidently, gesturing toward the huge red orb sinking ever lower over the treetops. "We'll start out in the morning."

"Very well." Adam couldn't help wondering how the position of the sun could do them any good, considering they had no way of knowing how far they might have wandered in that cave, or in which direction. Still, he reminded himself that Franklin had an uncanny way out here in the wilderness. He and Ellie would just have to trust him. What other option did they have, after all?

"There's not much time before it will be fully dark," Ellie said. "Adam, why don't you gather some branches or leaves so that we might sleep more comfortably in the mouth of the cave? I shall help Frank find us some food in the meantime."

At daybreak, they set out in the direction Franklin claimed would lead them back toward the Ohio River and, eventually, Pittsburgh. "It shall be a rather long walk," he warned. "We came a fair way underground."

"Never mind," Ellie replied. "The season is mild, and we are all young and strong. However long it takes, we shall get there eventually."

Adam forced a chuckle. "You are the cartographer in the family," he said. "I suppose you shall enjoy seeing more of this wild country and making your notes."

"Oh, that reminds me!" Ellie reached into her clothes and pulled out her diary. "I meant to describe the cave in my book. The pages got wet when we were in the river, but I think they are all right now."

She scribbled busily as they walked. Meanwhile, Adam's mind drifted back to his earlier thoughts of treasure. Now that he was almost positive the medallion was trying to lead him somewhere, he was more tempted than ever to delay their return to the East Coast. But he reminded himself that he could not. Perhaps he would return to Pittsburgh at a later time to follow those marks in the woods. For the moment, though, his only task was to keep his sister and Franklin safe and return them home.

For the next five or six days, Adam and his companions walked steadily throughout the daylight hours, stopping only occasionally to rest, eat, and drink. Amazingly, Franklin kept them fairly well fed on the wild stuff he gathered and even the occasional small animal or bird that he managed to capture in handmade traps. He was able to light fires every night that was not rainy, thanks to a bit of flint he discovered, and he had an unerring ear for the sound of streams running through the trees that provided their drinking water. He also managed to keep them free of any close encounters with natives or aggressive beasts, avoiding paths that showed the wear of human feet or the prints of any larger predators. Franklin further insisted on camping in sheltered areas at night.

"How did you come to know all this about surviving in the wilderness?" Adam asked the boy as he bit into the cooked flesh of a rabbit. "Was it all learned in those months we were in Pittsburgh? It seems near impossible you could have picked up so much on your own."

Franklin glanced at him, then down at the ground. "Me dad," he explained. "He grew up poor back in Ireland. From the time I can remember, he spoke of making the most of the land, finding food and exploring and such. S'pose it all stuck in me head even after he passed."

Adam didn't know what to say in reply to that, so he merely took another bite of the gamy meat. While chewing, he stole a glance over at the boy. Franklin was still staring at the ground with a small frown on his face. But the frown didn't seem directed at Adam. In fact, since entering that cave, their relations had truly changed for the better. Lately, the three of them—Adam, Franklin, Ellie—actually felt like a team.

A few more days passed. Adam didn't say anything to the others, but he was beginning to grow quite worried. They had already covered a much greater distance on this trek than they had underground; he was certain of it. Even if Franklin was aiming them farther upstream than where they'd last left the river, shouldn't they have arrived at its banks by now?

Adam spent much of the day trying to calculate the rate of travel of their journey downstream by boat versus the required time to cover the same distance on foot. He alternated this by then focusing more on the letter and its meaning. He even convinced Ellie to sketch out a *tabula recta* in her notebook and try some of the keywords they'd guessed back in the cave. But none turned up anything intelligible from the coded letter.

It was late afternoon when Ellie, who was walking a little ahead of the others at the moment, let out a cry. "The river!" she called out. "I hear it!"

"What?" Adam had been feeling weary after yet another full day of trudging through the forest. But at his sister's words, he flew forward with renewed energy. And finally he heard it too—the unmistakable sound of flowing water. "You did it, Franklin!" he exclaimed. "You got us back to the river!"

Franklin merely shrugged and scurried forward. Soon all three of them burst out onto the edge of a broad, muddy, languorously flowing river.

Ellie and Franklin let out whoops of triumph and joy and danced about on the shore. Adam joined in, though he couldn't help but feel a twinge of confusion. Why did the river seem so much wider and the water so much muddier than he recalled? Furthermore, why did they now find themselves standing on the opposite bank from where they'd started, judging by the direction of its flow?

Surely there's a logical reason, and I'd only look all the more foolish by asking the others, he thought with a quick glance at his overjoyed companions. *Perhaps that cave crossed beneath the river—it was certainly deep enough, I'd reckon—and took us far off to the east, and we have only now found our way back from that direction. . . . In any case, we are here now, and that is all that matters.*

Still, he found himself wishing that he'd paid more attention to all of Ellie's chatter about maps and directions and such throughout their lives. Living in populous and well-mapped Massachusetts, settled for nearly two hundred years now, he'd felt little need to develop such skills. But at the moment he would have welcomed such knowledge, if only so he would not be forced to follow the other two quite so blindly.

He kept such thoughts to himself, however. There was no sense in annoying Ellie or offending Franklin by implying that he did not trust their guidance. Surely this was the correct river before them. What else could it be?

After a brief rest, they started walking upstream along the riverside. "We should be able to go a few more miles by nightfall," Ellie said cheerfully.

"Indeed," Adam agreed wearily. "The farther we walk in each day, the sooner we can be home to rest our feet by the fireplace with some real food in our bellies."

As the light faded, they began to look around for a good camping spot. Franklin scouted a short distance farther upstream on his own, and after a minute or two let out a shout. "Look, is that a fire up ahead?"

Adam hurried after him and soon spotted the orange glow of firelight flickering through the trees just beyond the next bend of the river. "Come on!" he cried with a rush of excitement. "It has to be a house or a camp. We can ask for help from whoever is there!"

They rushed forward. It was almost fully dark by this time, making it rough going. As they drew closer to the glow of the fire, the trees and darkness still conspired to hide whoever or whatever lay ahead aside from the fire itself. But Adam glanced out toward the river and, in the last of the sun's rays, spotted a boat anchored just out from the firelight.

"Run ahead, Franklin," Ellie urged breathlessly at that moment. "Tell them we are coming!"

"No—wait." Adam grabbed the boy's shoulder before he could obey Ellie's request. "Hold on a moment. Doesn't that keelboat out there look a bit familiar?"

Ellie frowned. "Adam, what are you—" she began with a touch of impatience in her voice.

But Franklin's eyes widened as he glanced out toward the water. "Ssh!" he hushed Ellie. "He's right. It could be—them. Looks like the same boat."

"Stay here, both of you," Adam ordered in a whisper. "I shall go ahead and see."

He crept on through the forest, taking extra care now to make as little sound as possible. Soon he reached the edge of a clearing.

Within was a rough camp. And sitting beside the fire were the three Brewster brothers. They were arguing over something or other, but Adam didn't stick around to listen. As quickly and quietly as possible, he made his way back to the others.

They withdrew to a safe distance and discussed what to do. "What are the chances after how far we've come?" Ellie exclaimed, looking stricken. "How is it that we keep encountering this horrible trio everywhere we go? It seems utterly impossible!"

"It is really no great surprise. After all, we're all on the same river, aren't we?" Adam shrugged. Despite the obvious danger of having the Brewsters so close again, he actually felt reassured by seeing them. It meant that they were on the right track, after all. The detour involving the chase and then the cave must have taken them all farther downriver than they'd been before, that was all.

"We shall have to skirt around them," Ellie said with a sigh. "Go deep into the forest until we're sure we're well and truly past."

Adam smiled. "I have a better idea," he said. "Listen. . . ."

Thirteen

"The Brewsters are going to be furious when they awaken," Ellie said.

"Good. They deserve it." Adam grinned. He couldn't believe how smoothly his plan had gone—for once, luck seemed to be smiling upon them. A light rain had begun falling even as they had crept down the riverbank a few hours earlier, muffling any noise they might make as they carefully untied the Brewsters' keelboat, climbed aboard, and used the long poles aboard to push it away from shore through the shallows. When they judged they were far enough away that the additional sound wouldn't carry, they switched to the oars, rowing upstream, hugging the shore to avoid the strongest part of the current.

Meanwhile, Ellie had taken a look around the boat. In the small, rough cabin, she found a large quantity of food and other supplies.

"It is fortunate for us that they did not unload much

tonight," she said, peering into a tin of tea. "They must have planned to stay in that spot only until morning."

After that, they had spent several minutes gorging themselves on the supplies. They had eaten their fill of the Brewsters' stores of chipped beef, crackers, pretzels, pemmican, and even some preserved vegetables.

Now, with their stomachs more sated than they had been since leaving Pittsburgh many weeks ago, they were rowing and poling strongly upstream by the light of the moon. They didn't dare stop to rest, or even to put up the sails, until they'd put as much distance as possible between themselves and the now-stranded Brewsters. They'd discussed heading downriver instead, which would certainly be easier. But somewhat to Adam's surprise, it had taken little to convince the other two to pull upriver for Pittsburgh instead.

Now, despite all the obvious difficulties and dangers of their situation, Adam felt lighthearted and almost gleeful. Guiding their new boat upstream would be hard work indeed. But it would be worth it when they spotted the docks of Pittsburgh.

By midway through the following day, Adam was feeling a

bit less sanguine. He suspected his uncertain mood had something to do with lack of sleep and tired muscles. Still, as he glanced at the unfamiliar sights slowly sliding past on either side of them, he once again felt that wriggle of doubt within his mind. This time he couldn't resist sharing it.

"Listen, where do you think we are exactly?" he said. "Nothing we have passed looks the least bit familiar. . . . Could we be so much farther downstream than I had imagined?"

Ellie shrugged. "We did travel a long way in that cave and then later on foot," she said, apparently not interested in the subject. "But, listen—should we give that coded letter another try? I've thought of another possible key—it could be some combination of Jefferson's and Lewis's names. What do you think?"

"It seems worth a try," Adam replied absently, distracted by the sight of an odd-looking pyramidal mound off to the left. Surely he would have noticed *that* had he seen it before. . . .

He gradually put his worries out of his mind and focused once again on the treasure quest as Ellie scribbled in her notebook, trying every possible permutation of the two men's names. But, once again, they had no luck in decoding the letter.

Finally, Ellie blew her lips out in frustration, staring down at the page. "It is no good. I'm beginning to fear we'll never hit upon the key."

Franklin was working one of the poles as they maneuvered through some shallows along the river's edge. "Perhaps only Mr. Lewis can guess the key," he said. "Might be better to find him and ask it, mightn't it?"

"Very funny, Frank." Adam leaned over from his own rowing spot to take the letter from Ellie's hand. "No, there's got to be a way to figure it out. He wouldn't have sent it off to Lewis without even the slightest clue in how to decipher it, and even if they'd discussed it previously—"

Suddenly, Ellie gasped. "Give me that!" she cried excitedly, grabbing the letter back. She scanned it and broke into an exuberant grin. "That's it!" she cried. "Oh, that President Jefferson is a clever one. He gives us the key right here in the first part of the letter, see?"

Adam stopped rowing and scooted over to read the letter over her shoulder. He'd paid little attention to the noncoded part up until then, but now read it with more careful eyes.

Pursuant to my earlier letters, I now offer you this confidential missive that I am trustful you alone shall be capable of deciphering to your great fortune. Thus, with preamble, I offer you these key words.

"Key words," Adam said aloud as he scanned the last line. "Is that it? He is telling us he is offering us the 'key words.' Could the words of the note itself be the key?"

"Not quite!" Ellie's eyes were glowing. "At least I do not think so. Did you not notice that he says 'with preamble'? It should read '*without* preamble' to read correctly, and I cannot help but think that a learned man such as the president would not make such an error. I think the wording could be intentional."

"The Constitution!" Adam blurted out, thinking of the great political document that had been adopted when he and Ellie were mere infants. "That has a preamble, does it not? Perhaps we are meant to use that text as the key!" Then his heart sank. "However, I am afraid I do not know it."

"I do," Frank spoke up. At the others' surprised looks, he smiled proudly. "Mum said I had a head for words and numbers and such as that. I remember most everything I see or hear." He cleared his throat. "'We the people of the United States, in order to form a more perfect union . . .'"

"Hold it, that's enough. Let me try that much before you go on." Ellie busily bent over her notebook once again.

As she worked, Adam kept staring at the letter. Something about their solution was bothering him, but he wasn't certain what it might be.

Finally, Ellie looked up with a sigh. "No good," she said. "I've tried using the Preamble every which way. It doesn't spell out anything intelligible."

"Of course!" Adam blurted out, the answer finally clicking in his mind. "That's because we have the *wrong* preamble! This is President Thomas Jefferson we are talking about, yes? Unless I am misremembering what I have always heard, he had little to do with the creation of the Constitution. However, there is *another* important document with a preamble—one for which Mr. Jefferson was said to have been the primary author!"

Franklin gasped and smacked himself on the forehead. "The Declaration of Independence!" he cried. "I know that one, too."

He began to quote the second preamble. This time, Ellie

let him recite the entire first line, writing it down as fast as he said it.

> We hold these truths to be self-evident, that all men are created equal, that they are endowed by their Creator with certain unalienable Rights, that among these are Life, Liberty and the pursuit of Happiness.

"That should be enough," Adam said before Frank could continue, barely remembering to continue rowing so that they didn't start drifting back downstream with the current. "The cipher isn't very long, after all. Try again using that as the key, Ellie." He felt a tightening in his gut telling him that they had the right answer this time—that deep-belly certainty, his father had always jokingly called it. Now, finally, Adam knew exactly what he meant.

Ellie's pencil flew over the paper. After only a moment, she let out a cry. "It's working! See? I have the first two words already: Only one."

"Keep going," Adam urged. He glanced over at Frank, whose eyes were wide and excited.

Ellie nodded and bent over her notebook again. Nobody spoke for several minutes as she worked, matching each letter of the coded message with one from the key phrase and thereby locating each decoded letter on the *tabula recta* she'd written out. Adam was itching to move closer and help, but he knew he was needed at the oar.

Finally, his sister looked up. "I've got the whole thing," she said. "I'm not sure what it means, but at least it's a legible sentence. Here."

She handed the notebook over to Adam. He stopped rowing for a moment and looked at it, holding it out a bit so Franklin could see as well. The message she had decoded was not very long.

Only one of fifty-six holds the key;
Beg ye the secret of C.C. of C.

"What does that mean?" Franklin's forehead crinkled in confusion.

Adam grinned. "This reminds me of the stories Father

tells of the days when he tracked down those munitions for the Revolution," he said to Ellie. "Remember? That quest had just this sort of cryptic clue, which he and Uncle Duncan and their friend George then had to sort out, each one leading to . . ."

His voice faded away as they rounded a curve of the river and suddenly came within view of a tall limestone bluff with numerous buildings atop it. Adam blinked, wondering if his eyes were deceiving him.

"Do you see that?" he asked.

Ellie and Franklin exchanged a look. "I think—I think it may be, er . . ." Ellie stammered.

"What?" Adam turned to stare at her. "What is it, Ellie? You look very odd all of a sudden."

She hesitated, glancing once more at Franklin, who shrugged. "It is St. Louis, Adam," she said at last. "I believe that is the settlement of St. Louis just ahead."

"What?" Adam's head spun. "Is this some sort of joke? How can that be St. Louis?"

Ellie's eyes filled with tears. "I'm sorry, Adam!" she cried. "All along, we have intentionally been leading you the wrong way, trying to come here to find Lewis and Clark. We agreed to keep it from you because we knew you would never agree to the plan."

Adam's jaw dropped and the oar he was holding almost followed. "Of course I would not agree!" he exclaimed. "Have I not been trying this whole time to get us back to Pittsburgh and then home?"

"Yes, but now that we have the clue, the treasure . . ." Franklin began.

"It doesn't matter!" Adam grabbed the nearest pole and dug it into the riverbed, single-handedly turning them in to the shoreline sloping down to meet the water—the water of the Mississippi River and not the Ohio, as he now realized. As soon as he felt the keel hit bottom, he leaped out, not minding that his clothes were instantly soaked. He had to get away for a moment—had to figure out what to think and to feel.

For the truth was—although his primary reaction was of betrayal—he was also feeling the stirrings of gladness. But no! He shook off the latter sentiment, focusing on the former. They had lied to him. They had schemed and plotted, and thanks to his own hopelessness with directions, he had allowed it to happen. How could he have been so foolish?

"Adam!" Ellie was splashing through the shallows after him, holding up her skirts. "Please, let me explain."

He glanced back at her. By now the tears were streaming down her cheeks. "Explain? How are you going to explain *this*?" He jerked one hand to indicate St. Louis just ahead.

"It is just that I—I wanted this adventure more than anything in my life," she said, choking back a sob. "I was willing to risk life and limb for it. But I never realized that I might also be risking your good feelings. Franklin was sure you would come around eventually, but I suppose I should have known better."

"So this was Frank's idea, was it?" Adam shot a sour look at the boy, who was struggling to guide the keelboat the rest of the way to shore on his own.

"No!" Ellie protested. Then she paused. "Well—yes, I suppose in the beginning it was. But he only suggested it because he knew what I wanted." She shrugged. "And of course, he was hoping for the chance to find more of those medallion clues. He thinks we are traveling in the right direction for that. You know, he is so much interested in treasure, one might almost think his last name should be Gates."

She smiled slightly at that. But Adam merely shook his head, recalling all the times Ellie and Franklin had wandered off together—merely gathering food, he'd thought. Now he realized they must have been discussing this plan of theirs every time he was out of earshot.

"I cannot believe this," he said coldly. "We have gone weeks in the wrong direction. By my judgment, it must be at least late May by now—we'll be lucky if we can find passage back home before next winter arrives, especially with no money left to pay our way. I never would have expected this sort of irresponsible behavior of you, Ellie!"

No, the thought entered his mind before he could stop it. *I would have expected it from me.*

That much was true enough. He'd always been the easygoing one, the one who took life as it came and didn't worry about much. All that had changed on this journey. Or had it? True, he was angry with Ellie and Franklin for deceiving him all this time. But shouldn't he also be angry with himself? After all, he'd just flowed along as he'd always done, almost as lazy and unthinking as the river itself, following the path of least resistance while entertaining vague daydreams of following in his father's footsteps in search of treasure. Now, looking back, he saw that there was so much that he could have done differently. . . .

"Hey!" Franklin shouted from some distance away.

Adam glanced over, fearing that the boy had lost control of the keelboat. The last thing they needed was to have it float off without them. At least perhaps they would be able to trade it and its supplies for a little money toward those coach fares.

But Franklin had already tied the boat to a stout tree on shore and was now picking his way up the bank toward another large pyramidal mound like the one Adam had noticed earlier.

"What is it now?" Adam muttered, feeling little patience at the moment for the boy's antics. "Come back here, Frank. We need to get to the settlement up ahead and start figuring out what to do next."

"But see, here it is!" Franklin had just reached the base of the mound. He jumped up and down and waved his arms, sounding excited. "Right here on this thing!"

He wouldn't stop shouting and pointing until Adam and Ellie finally climbed up to see what he was showing them. When he reached the base of the mound, Adam stared in shock at what he saw there.

"Is that—it's the picture from the medallion!" he exclaimed, all other thought fleeing his mind as he stared in wonder at the familiar image, carved in a most unfamiliar location. "How can it be?"

"See? It is pointing north-northwest—directly up the river." Franklin grinned. "All we need to do is follow it to find the treasure!"

Adam gazed at the timeworn markings without answering for a long moment. Once again, he was getting that sensation in his gut—the deep-belly certainty. It seemed that they really were on the trail of the medallion now, wherever it might be leading. And now that they'd figured out Jefferson's coded letter as well . . .

He glanced over and found Ellie and Franklin both staring at him wordlessly. Ellie's eyes were filled with pleading, Franklin's with challenge.

"Well?" Ellie said. "What do you think, Adam? If you wish, we can go on up to St. Louis and see about arranging transport home."

"But—" Franklin began.

Ellie shushed him with a look. "It is Adam's decision,"

she said simply. "It was wrong of us to deceive him, and he deserves our respect now at the very least."

Adam could tell that she meant it this time. He knew that Ellie, at least, would abide by whatever decision he made now—to return home, or to continue the adventure from here.

He glanced from the symbol on the mound to the notebook in Ellie's hand to the settlement just upstream. Then he took a deep breath, hoping he wasn't making another mistake.

"Let's leave the boat here and walk the rest of the way to St. Louis," he said firmly.

Ellie's face fell. "Very well," she said softly. Frank frowned but didn't speak.

"The distance isn't far," Adam said. "It should be easy enough to carry the supplies we'll need back here on foot."

"The . . . the supplies?" Ellie echoed uncertainly.

"Of course." Adam smiled at her. "You don't think we're going to set off up the river into the uncharted wilderness with only what we have on the boat right now, do you? That would be downright irresponsible."

Fourteen

Less than three days later they were under way once again, poling their way up the Mississippi. Following the markings, they headed north toward the river's confluence with the Missouri.

They had spent the intervening time in St. Louis, a bustling and surprisingly well-provided settlement of around one thousand citizens that boasted a doctor, a couple of taverns, and several blacksmiths. The visitors also had their choice of grocers ready to sell them supplies at astoundingly high prices, though luckily one of them was willing to trade his stock for Ellie's gold ring as well as some unneeded items the Brewsters had left aboard the keelboat. While in town, Ellie also confirmed that Lewis and Clark and their group had, indeed, embarked upriver from their winter camp about two weeks earlier.

"Never mind," Ellie told Adam and Franklin cheerfully after receiving the news. "I am sure they will be stopping frequently to record what they see along the way. With any luck, we should be able to catch them before long."

"I would hope so," Adam said, kneeling in the center of the boat to adjust the sail, which was just beginning to catch a breeze. "It would be safer to travel with the group."

"Indeed," Ellie agreed. "Until we find them, we shall have to be extracautious about wild beasts, such as bears."

Adam nodded. "True. But those are not the beasts I was referring to," he said. "I was thinking of the Brewsters. Surely, they now think us dead in that fire and have no idea that it was we who absconded with their boat and supplies. But should we encounter them again . . ."

Ellie shuddered. "I think I would prefer to encounter the wild beasts."

"Still, we don't need no one else," Franklin spoke up from his spot at the rudder. "Else we'll have to share the treasure."

Ellie sighed. "Oh, dear," she said. "So it's true, then. The treasure illness is catching."

Adam just grinned. He still wasn't completely certain it had been the right decision to continue on up to the Missouri instead of heading for home. But after seeing that marking on the mound outside of town, he had been unable to resist. Besides, both Franklin and Ellie seemed excited and content with the prospect of the coming adventure.

We have come this far, after all, he thought, leaning back to yank the sail into place as the wind did its best to snatch it away. *Why not press on and see what we can find?*

They had made it to the Missouri and been working their way up the river for just over a week when the keelboat ran aground on a shallow mound of sand in its path. All three of them tried to push it free with the poles and oars as was usual with such an occurrence. But for once, this method failed.

"Blazes!" Adam exclaimed. "Well, it is a hot day—I suppose it shall feel rather good to get wet."

He lowered himself off the side of the boat into the water, which flowed swiftly around his waist. Franklin jumped in as well.

"What shall I do?" Ellie asked, kneeling at the edge of the boat. "Do you need me to push, as well?"

"No, you stay at the rudder and prepare to steer," Adam said. "Frank and I will see if we can jar it loose."

It took several tries, a skinned shoulder, and a lot of

muttering. But finally, the two of them managed to rock the boat hard enough to set it free. The keelboat jolted and bucked its way off the sandbar.

"That's it!" Ellie cried, holding on as the boat rocked wildly to right itself in the water.

Adam hoisted himself back aboard. Franklin did the same. But the boy paused with one foot still dangling into the water, staring wide-eyed at something behind Adam.

"Oi!" the boy cried. "Our food!"

Glancing back, Adam was just in time to see the wooden crate that held most of their food supplies skidding across the far end of the boat. He realized that Ellie must have been taking something out of it when they had run aground. And now the force of freeing the boat was sending the crate sliding right off the edge.

SPLASH!

The supplies landed in the water and then bobbed to the surface. Instantly, the strong river current caught the crate and spun it away from the boat, dragging it out toward the middle of the river.

"Oh, no!" Ellie cried. "Nearly all our food is in there. What shall we do without it? Oh, but this is all my fault;

I should have secured it better—"

"Never mind." Adam bit his lip, his heart sinking as he watched the crate float farther away. "We survived with hardly any supplies before; we can do it again. Besides, once we catch up to Captain Lewis's party we shan't have to worry. They have plenty of supplies."

The words were hardly out of his mouth when there was another splash. "Frank!" Ellie cried.

Glancing over, Adam saw that the boy had leaped back into the river and was now swimming after the crate. He caught up to it within a few strokes and clung to it, turning back to the boat.

"Go, Frank!" Adam cheered.

But his grin faded quickly. Franklin was struggling against the current. As they watched, he lost ground and began to be pulled downstream.

"The river is carrying him away!" Ellie cried. "The current is too much for him—he's too small!"

"Hold the rudder steady, Ellie," Adam told her grimly. Without waiting for a response, he pushed off and dove into the water. The current with him, Adam quickly reached the boy's side. He grabbed Franklin by the arm.

"Hold on to the crate, and kick!" he shouted, spitting foul-tasting river water out of his mouth.

Then he turned and, using his one free arm as well as his legs, struck out for the keelboat. It was slow going, and his muscles soon burned from the effort. But he kept on, and finally they escaped from the worst of the current, coming into a calmer patch of water where the keelboat was bobbing. He was able to let go of Franklin, and the two of them swam the rest of the way with the crate between them. Ellie was waiting to pull the crate back on board and help them up.

"Oh, I am so glad you are safe!" she cried, enveloping Adam in a hug without minding that he was soaked. Then she turned to hug Franklin, as well. "*Both* of you! Do not scare me like that again, all right?"

Over Ellie's shoulder, Franklin shot Adam a weak smile—and a look of grudging respect. "I won't, Miss Ellie," he mumbled. "Thank you, Mr. Adam."

Adam nodded wearily, leaning back against the shelter to catch his breath. "You are welcome, Frank."

"Fifty-six," Adam mused, staring at the president's letter, which was beginning to look rather frayed about the edges, as the keelboat was carried upriver by a stiff breeze. "Do you suppose that could refer to the population of a settlement somewhere along this river?"

Another week or more has passed, and they were making slow, but steady, progress up the Missouri. At first they had passed settlements regularly, but it had been some time now since they had seen any sign of human habitation on the wild, wooded river shore aside from the occasional fur trader or other travelers who had passed on their way downstream. They had not yet caught sight of Lewis and Clark's expedition, though they'd seen some evidence that the group had passed this way before them—an abandoned shoe here, some footprints on the shore there, and other similar clues. One of the fur traders, as well, had stopped to chat and confirmed that he'd passed that party upriver about a week previously.

Now Ellie looked up from her notebook, where she was recording her thoughts on the trees, insects, and fish they had spotted along the way. "I have not given it much thought since our last discussion," she admitted in response to Adam's query. "There is so much to see, it is filling up my mind to overflowing!"

Adam was glad that she was finding their journey so rewarding. Life on the river was strenuous and uncomfortable compared to their everyday life. But he had to admit he was enjoying it, too. It was like nothing he had ever experienced before.

Still, he knew he would not be truly satisfied with this adventure unless he could crack the mystery of those decoded lines. Hoping to refocus Ellie's sharp mind onto the problem, he repeated his question now that he had her attention.

"The population of a settlement?" She looked dubious. "It seems unlikely. That number would be far too likely to change—through births, deaths, comings, and goings. A village that numbered fifty-six souls one week might be sixty the next and forty-seven the one after that."

"Yes, you are right." Adam sighed and scratched his head. It was a hot day, and the gnats and flies were bothersome. "Only one of fifty-six . . . only one of fifty-six . . . What significance could there be to that number? Frank? What do you think?"

"Huh?" The boy looked up. He was sitting near the rudder, steering when needed and otherwise playing with the sheet of paper that had his drawing of the medallion marks.

"We were just trying to figure out this clue to the treasure," Adam explained, holding up the letter.

Franklin shrugged. "What's it matter?" he said. "We got all we need for now from the medallion thing."

Indeed, they had seen several other markers over the weeks since they'd left St. Louis—one had been a carving on a steep, rocky part of the riverbank, easily visible even from out on the water. Another had marked a large stone at a spot where a tributary flowed off to one side, clearly marking the way forward on the main river. Yet another had been barely visible, carved into an ancient, rotting stump that had once been an enormous tree—only Franklin's sharp eyes had spotted that one. It was becoming clear that whoever had created the medallion and laid the trail had clearly followed the same river they were on now, leaving a mark at any spot where the correct way forward might be questionable.

"I know, and that is indeed showing us the way thus far," Adam said. "But we still do not know whether the medallion and this letter are both leading to the same treasure or two completely different ones. If they *are* part of the same trail, surely we are meant to figure out both clues to reach the ultimate goal, don't you think?" Adam glanced down again at the letter, troubled once more by something that had occurred to him more often lately. "This message seems to indicate that there is a further key needed to acquire what we seek—'only one of fifty-six holds the key.' Are we going to track down the treasure only to find that we lack the key to open wherever it might be hidden? Or to be missing some final clue or key to show us the exact spot?"

Franklin shrugged again. But Ellie looked concerned.

"The clue *does* seem to indicate something of the sort, doesn't it?" she said. "Still, I suppose all we can do is keep trying to solve the riddle, and then if nothing comes of it, see what we need to do after."

"Yes, I suppose you are right," Adam agreed. Still, he couldn't help suppress a stirring of unease as he glanced down once more at the letter.

Several days later, they stopped to make camp in a pleasant area of flat ground and forest punctuated by open, grassy areas. There, in a sparsely wooded spot, they found both raspberries and mulberries in great abundance. Even as the light began to fade from the sky, Ellie and Franklin set out in one direction, eating their way along, but Adam decided to wander the other way, hoping for privacy to relieve himself. He forgot that need for a while as he came upon yet another batch of berries. After gorging himself on the sweet fruit, he wandered on, trying to determine whether or not it was worth returning to camp for a container to pick more berries for breakfast.

It was only when he came to a clearing on the bank of a small, rushing tributary that he remembered that he still hadn't attended to his bladder. Quickly doing so, he realized the sun had dipped behind the horizon and it was rapidly turning to dusk. Rearranging his clothing, he turned in preparation of heading back to the spot where he'd left the others.

But he had barely taken two steps in that direction when one of the shadows beneath the trees seemed to move and separate from the others. Adam froze as a lean, gray shape crept out into the fading light of the clearing. It was a wolf! They had often heard the wild creatures howling at night, though up to this point they had seen them only infrequently and at a distance.

Now he was close enough to stare into the creature's eerie gold eyes. The wolf licked its muzzle and lowered its head, as if trying to determine whether or not Adam might be edible.

Adam could do nothing but stare back at the wolf, too terrified to move or even think.

Within seconds, several more wolves had materialized out of the darkness to join the first. The largest of them stepped forward, its nose twitching curiously.

This is it, Adam thought bleakly. *Whoever would have guessed it—a civilized town boy bred and raised, fated to meet my end in the midst of an untamed wilderness at the jaws of these ferocious beasts. I wonder if Ellie and Frank will ever even find my remains. . . .*

As if summoned by his very thought, Franklin suddenly appeared at that moment at the edge of the clearing just a few yards away from the wolves. Suddenly frightened as much for the boy as for himself, Adam began to wave his hands at Franklin.

"Go!" he called hoarsely. "Get out of here before they see you!"

Franklin blinked at him, then glanced over at the wolves. Instead of freezing or running or shrieking in fear, as Adam might have expected, the boy instantly dropped to his knees and started scrabbling about on the ground.

What in blazes is he doing? Adam wondered.

He had his answer a moment later. One of the wolves had just turned and taken a step toward Franklin when the boy sprang to his feet, both hands loaded with stones.

"Go on!" he shouted at the top of his lungs, flinging one of the stones at the nearest creature. "Get out of here, you mongrels! Go!"

He hopped up and down, throwing his rocks one by one and waving his arms over his head in between tosses. The wolves froze for a moment, seemingly startled. Then, as if at some invisible signal among themselves, they all faded back into the woods.

Adam slumped with relief, his hands shaking. "Frank," he croaked as the boy came toward him. "What—why—how did you know what to do to chase them off like that?"

"Wolves are shy of humans," Franklin explained. "Found that out when I was exploring 'round Pittsburgh last fall and winter. Lots of wolves about out there, too." He shrugged. "They don't usually want no quarrel if you're loud enough about it." His serious little face suddenly cracked into a sly smile. "Leastways, not the ones I met so far. Then again, maybe those ones just weren't real hungry."

Somehow, the comment struck Adam as the funniest he'd heard in a while. He smiled, then chuckled . . . then found himself laughing so hard that it hurt. Collapsing onto the ground, he laughed and laughed and then laughed some more. After a moment, Franklin began to laugh along with him.

Finally, exhausted, Adam rolled over to look at the boy. "We shouldn't tell Ellie about this."

Franklin looked thoughtful, then shook his head. "Nope," he agreed. "She don't need to know. She's right fond of you, and it'll worry her to hear of it." The sly smile appeared again. "Besides, she'll only want to stay here to track down them wolves and sketch 'em, won't she? And then we'll never get to that treasure."

Adam grinned. "Did anyone ever tell you you're a true student of human nature, Franklin Poole?"

"Eh?" Franklin looked perplexed, then shrugged. "Come on, Mr. Adam. We better get back and check on Ellie. There's wild beasts about, you know."

"I know." Adam climbed to his feet and clapped the boy

on the shoulder. For once, Franklin didn't shy away from his touch. "And you can drop the mister, by the way. Just call me Adam, all right?"

The boy shot him a look, then smiled rather shyly. "All right . . . er, *Adam*." And for the first time, when he said it, there was not the slightest bit of disrespect.

Fifteen

As the weeks passed, Adam, Ellie, and Frank grew accustomed to their new, transient way of life. They took turns at poling or rowing when there was an opposing breeze or none at all, and at working the sail when the wind was at their backs. Progress upstream was laboriously slow, but none of them minded much. The leisurely pace allowed Ellie more time to sketch new flora and fauna on the ever-changing shores and work on the maps she was making of the river.

Adam and Frank, meanwhile, kept a close lookout for more of the medallion markings leading them toward what they hoped would be a vast treasure. In most cases, they found one wherever the river split or there was otherwise a question of how to proceed onward, though in a few cases there was none to be seen—perhaps erased by the passage of time—and they had to guess. In those latter cases, they were always a bit anxious and on edge until the next marker appeared to show that they'd made the correct choice.

They saw no other humans except a fur trader or two in passing. However, they did continue to see evidence that the Lewis and Clark expedition was still ahead of them, though they never seemed to get close enough to see or hear the other party.

"It is strange," Ellie mused one day as she sketched a buffalo she had seen on an island they had passed earlier. "They have no idea that we are following them, and yet we are aware of them at all times."

Adam stared out at the prairie land they were passing through. The grasses were beginning to look dry and brown as the late-summer sun baked them with its heat.

"Indeed," he said. "We seem to be gaining some ground on them; I'd guess we are probably only two or three days behind by now. I suppose if there were a great need, we could exert enough effort to catch up to them at any time."

"Don't want to catch them," Franklin spoke up. He grinned at Adam. "Remember? More treasure for us."

Adam grinned back. Turning to glance at the shoreline again, he spied an area of steep bluffs just ahead. It looked like a good spot to check for a marker. Each time they spotted another, faded from age and the elements, Adam couldn't help feeling a quiver of doubt about their quest. The more time passed, the more firmly Franklin seemed to believe that they were on the trail of the same treasure alluded in President Jefferson's letter. But what if the truth was what Adam had previously assumed—that the prize they were chasing by following those marks had nothing to do with the Treasure of the Ancients at all? What if it was an entirely different treasure—one so old it had crumbled into dust or ceased to be valuable?

Grandfather says that's what happened to our ancestor who passed down the medallion, he reminded himself. *He thought he would find a glorious store of Spanish gold or other great riches, but instead it is said that he uncovered only a bunch of dusty old native headdresses and that sort of thing. And the medallion is said to date from the same era as that so-called treasure. . . .*

He bit his lip, trying to banish such thoughts as he turned his mind to the decoded letter. After all, it had to mean something, whether connected to the medallion or not. And a man such as President Jefferson surely wouldn't bother to go to such lengths for anything but a truly valuable treasure . . . would he?

* * *

Eventually the nights began to grow cooler, though the days remained warm enough to be plagued with mosquitoes and other flying pests. The river passed out of the area of woods and plains into an immense, hilly prairie dotted with vast herds of grazing creatures. Ellie was kept busy exclaiming over each new and interesting species—elk, buffalo, deer, antelopes, and many others—and making copious notes in her book.

As Adam watched her sketching a stout little furry creature that she said was known to the trappers as a prairie dog, he realized that no matter what came of this journey in the end, he was glad his sister had had the chance to make her dreams come true. For her, just being here—seeing these new sights and creatures and plants with her own eyes, sketching them with her own hand—was treasure enough.

On the topic of treasure, Adam continued pondering the clue in the letter, drawing Ellie and Franklin into his speculations whenever possible. One day they discussed the matter while Ellie sorted through the remaining supplies, trying to estimate how much longer they would last. Adam sat at the rudder steering the boat, which was being carried upriver by a stiff breeze with more than a hint of winter's coming chill behind it.

"I still think that if we can deduce what is meant by that number fifty-six, we shall be able to figure out the rest of the clue and how it might relate to the medallion, if at all," Adam mused.

"You may be right." Ellie tapped her fingers on the edge of the supply crate. "Fifty-six, fifty-six—let us think of possible explanations. Could it be a year? Did something of note happen in 1756, perhaps?"

"You know I have little memory for history." Adam glanced at Franklin, who was sprawled out poking at a bug crawling on the floor of the boat. "Frank, what do you know of the year 1756?"

"Eh?" Franklin looked up and blinked. "What d'you mean?" Once they'd explained it to him, he shrugged. "Seven Years' War began in 1756, I b'lieve. But that's not what I'd think of for the number fifty-six, where Mr. Jefferson's involved."

Adam gasped, the boy's comment triggering the answer in his mind. "Of course!" he shouted so loudly that his voice echoed off the bluffs they were passing. "Fifty-six—the

Declaration of Independence—why didn't we see it before?"
Ellie still looked confused, so he explained: "There were
fifty-six signers of the Declaration. Fifty-six!"

"Ah!" Ellie's expression cleared. But then she frowned.
"So which signer is indicated by C.C. of C.?"

"That I do not know," Adam admitted. "The only sign-
ers whose names I can recall offhand are President Adams,
President Jefferson himself, and the late Mr. Benjamin
Franklin."

"There was the esteemed Mr. Samuel Adams of
Boston," Ellie put in. "But none of them have the initials
C.C. I suppose it must be one of the signers from
Connecticut? That is surely the meaning of the third C."

Franklin was shaking his head. "No, no," he scolded
them. "The answer is obvious. C.C. of C. in relation to
the Declaration must indicate Mr. Charles Carroll of
Carrollton."

Both Gates twins turned to stare at him in surprise.
"Who?" Adam said.

The boy sighed loudly, picking at a splinter on the
boat's side with his grubby fingernails. "Charles Carroll
of Carrollton. The wealthy former senator from Maryland.

He was a signer of the Declaration."

"How do you know all that?" Ellie asked in wonder.

"Told you. I remember things." Franklin smiled. "Anyway, I grew up in Washington's city, remember? Not far from Maryland. Guess I just heard his name about often enough to recall it. It's good to notice every detail."

That much was true, Adam realized with some chagrin. He could certainly take a lesson from the boy about that. Perhaps if he'd paid more attention to detail himself, some of their tribulations on this trip might have been averted.

But this was no time to think of such things. Not now, when there were much more pressing matters to consider.

"All right, then," he said. "So if C.C. of C. is indeed referring to this Charles Carroll of Carrollton, then where does that leave us?" He frowned. "Were we meant to retrieve some sort of key from him in Maryland before commencing this quest?"

"It is probably not that at all," Ellie said. "Perhaps you shall merely need Mr. Carroll's name to solve some further clue later."

Franklin nodded. "If we have missed this key, so has Cap'n Lewis," he pointed out. "After all, this letter never reached him, thanks to them Brewster brothers."

"Indeed," Adam agreed. But he couldn't help feeling troubled by this strange new development, which seemed to raise more questions than it answered.

The farther they traveled, the more the weather began to shift over toward winter. The nights were growing quite cold now, and the leaves were beginning to drift from the trees. One day snow even flurried from the sky, though it did not stick to the ground. Adam alternated pondering the meaning of the Charles Carroll reference with worrying over whether they would reach some conclusion to this quest— or catch Lewis and Clark—before the weather prevented them from continuing any farther. He did not want to end up out in this wilderness alone for an entire winter. It would surely mean death.

One chilly afternoon, Franklin spotted another medallion marking on a large rock just above the waterline at river's edge. "Looks odd," he said, kneeling close to the edge of the keelboat and peering toward shore. "Can't really see which way the arrow is pointing."

"Might not be an arrow at all," Adam said. "It's not as if

there's any doubt about which way to go—the river is fairly straight here, and there are no tributaries that I can see."

Ellie glanced up from her notebook. "That rock is probably covered with water when the river is higher," she pointed out. "Some of the markings could have worn away over the years."

Adam nodded. "On the one hand, I can understand why whoever laid this trail chose this rock—the land near here offers few other visible spots for such a mark." He cast a glance at the cottonwood trees and grasses lining the banks. "On the other hand, why place a mark here at all?"

Franklin was still staring at the faded mark. "It looks different somehow," he murmured. "Not just the arrow. Need to see it closer."

"Very well. It is nearly time to stop and make camp anyway. We might as well put in here as anywhere else." Adam grabbed the sail.

As soon as they were close enough, Franklin leaped out of the boat and waded toward the marked rock, not seeming to mind the cold water. Adam called to him, asking for help with the boat, but the boy didn't answer or give any sign that he'd heard as he ran his thin fingers over the notches in the stone. With a resigned shrug, Adam hopped out himself, pulling the keelboat to shore and tying it to a tree. Then he and Ellie climbed the bank to start scouting a spot to camp.

They wandered about, not feeling in any particular hurry, as the sun had only just begun its march toward the horizon. However, Adam couldn't help noticing that the air was already cooling considerably as evening approached. Soon it would begin to snow, and ice would form on the river, making passage much more difficult. . . .

Suddenly, a sharp bang rang out like a sudden clap of thunder, so loud that it made both Adam and Ellie jump. It echoed across the open land and bounced off the bluffs on the other side of the river.

Ellie gasped. "Was that a gunshot?"

"It was." Adam's heart pounded as he realized what this meant. "I think we've finally nearly caught up with Lewis and Clark's men!"

"Come." Ellie turned, lifted her skirts, and ran full-out back toward the river's edge. "There is still daylight left. Perhaps by tonight we can be with them!"

Adam thought briefly of the treasure, and what it would mean were they to find it as part of the expedition rather than on their own. But after so many months of physical struggle and hardship, the thought of the relative ease of being part of a larger group was stronger than his desire not to share the treasure. He raced after his sister with a smile on his face at the thought of sitting beside a warm fire that he hadn't had to build himself, eating food that someone else had caught or prepared, hearing new stories from companions and knowing that from now on, he no longer had to feel responsible for everything that happened.

They soon reached the boat, still bobbing against its tie in the shallows. But there was no sign of Franklin.

"Frank!" Adam bellowed eagerly. "Ahoy! Come on, we have to hurry!"

There was no answer. Ellie tried calling as well, but she too was greeted only with the whisper of the wind through the grasses. The twins spent a good fifteen minutes wandering up and down the shoreline calling and searching. Still, there was no sign of Franklin.

Finally, Adam let out a sigh of frustration. "It is no use. Had he been close enough to hear, he would have answered by now." He frowned, adding in a matter, "If he had any intention to do so, that is."

Some of the familiar irritation with Franklin flowed back. *Why did he have to choose this moment to run off?* he thought. *Now we shall most likely have to wait until morning to set out, and if the expedition does the same, it may take longer yet to catch them. If only Frank could have stayed where we left him for once!*

"I hope he is all right," Ellie commented, unaware of her twin's thoughts—so unlike her own. "There are a great many wild beasts and other dangers about; just yesterday I spied a pack of smaller wolflike creatures skulking about on the shore as we were passing in broad daylight."

Adam shivered. And it was only at that moment that he recognized the truth. His mood had turned sour not because he was annoyed with Franklin for running off—it was because he was worried about him. It was the feeling he would have if he'd returned to find Ellie missing.

Well, what about that? he thought with wonder. *I suppose it is true. The three of us have become like a little family during this journey.*

He had plenty of time to ponder that, as Franklin didn't reappear until just before dark. At that time he rushed into camp, covered in dirt and wearing an expression of such glee and excitement that Adam instantly forgot that he'd meant to scold him soundly for disappearing.

"I found it!" Franklin cried, waving something in the air. "I found it!"

"What?" Ellie dropped the dry, brown grass she was using to build a campfire and rushed over. "Found what, Frank?"

Adam reached over and grabbed the object out of the boy's hand. It appeared to be some sort of cured animal pelt, crinkly and darkened with age. He stared at the black markings on it for a moment, not understanding.

"It's a map!" Franklin exclaimed. "See? I followed that marking by the river, and I found this. I think it's a treasure map!"

Sixteen

All three of them spoke at once. Finally, though, Adam silenced the other two and managed to get the story out of Franklin. The boy had examined the marking on the rock closely enough to notice an additional mark just below, nearly worn away by years of flowing water. It showed an odd series of bumps with a distinctly crooked one in the middle.

Sure enough, when Adam followed the boy down to the water's edge, he was just able to discern the faded mark in the dimming light. "See here?" Franklin traced the shallow groove with one finger. "There's this odd bumpy one right here in the middle with this oval-shaped thing just below it. So I went looking for something that looked like that. Found it straight in from here—bunch of hills with that funny one in the middle, just like this drawing."

"And this map was there?" Adam glanced at the animal skin in his hand. "Just like that?"

Franklin shrugged. "Had to dig for it." He held up his hands, which were coated with dirt. "Saw an oval rock that was shaped just like the marking. Moved it aside, and dug underneath. Found an old metal box with the map inside."

Ellie's eyes were wide with amazement. "I can hardly believe it," she exclaimed. "Can we really have stumbled upon a treasure out here in the middle of the wilderness?"

Adam was amazed, too. "Not just stumbled, Ellie. You know, you are really something, Franklin," he told the boy sincerely. "Despite the Gates family tradition of hunting for treasure, *you* have been the one doing most of the hard work on this quest."

Franklin shrugged. "Nah, not me," he mumbled shyly. "I'da not even known that letter had nothing to do with treasure if it weren't for you. All I been doing is helping you get through the wilderness and letting you do the decoding and such."

"That's not true." Ellie smiled and put an arm around his shoulders, not seeming to mind the dirt. "You were the one who could quote the preamble to help us with the cipher, and it was also you who knew the identity of C.C. of C. Not to mention figuring out the meaning of this marking after finding that first mark in the woods near Pittsburgh to start with."

"Come on," Adam said, starting back up the hill. "Let's go back to camp. It's getting too dark to see much, and I want to examine the map. Perhaps we'll be able to track down the treasure in the morning."

They wandered back up to their camp. The temperature had dropped since sunset, but Ellie had the fire nearly prepared and within minutes they were gathered around its warmth.

"Now, then." Adam spread the map over his knees, peering at it in the flickering light. "Let's see what we can make of this."

The other two bent in from either side to look. "Well, that is almost certainly meant to signify the river," Ellie said, pointing to the curving line that meandered up through the map.

"And that there looks to be mountains." Franklin jabbed a finger at some pointy triangles at the lower left corner of the map. "See? That part's darker than the rest."

"And it's marked with that same odd little figure from the medallion," Adam said, noting the humanlike figure with the six slashes through it drawn over the mountains. "Interesting. What do you suppose that means?"

Ellie shook her head. "I do not know. But judging by the shape of the river, this map seems to cover an extraordinarily large area." She leaned closer for a better look. "However, look at this—I recognize that series of curves. It's the section of river we have just traveled. Which means that we are here—just by this X by these other markings right there near the top. Do you suppose that X could mark the location of this possible treasure?"

Adam was impressed by her insights. *It is a good thing Ellie never listened to our relatives and all the others who said that there was no point in a young lady wasting her time with maps and such,* he thought with a smile.

"I think you could be right," he agreed. "How far do you estimate the X spot to be from here?"

"It is difficult to tell," Ellie answered. "Perhaps half a day's journey upriver?"

Franklin's face brightened. "Then we could find the treasure tomorrow, and then go looking for those other people afterward," he said. "They'd never have to know we found it 'less we tell them!"

Adam grinned. "True enough," he agreed. "But what if the treasure consists of a thousand enormous chests filled with gold and jewels? We might have to spend some of our newfound wealth to hire Lewis and Clark and their men to carry it back to the East Coast for us!"

He and Franklin were laughing at that when Ellie suddenly shushed them. "Did you hear that?" she asked.

"What?" Adam asked.

But then he heard it, too—human voices. They were coming from the direction of the river.

He gasped, jumping to his feet with the map still clutched in one hand. "It must be Lewis's men," he exclaimed. "Come, let's go see!"

They rushed for the riverbank. But when they crested the hill that brought them within view, they stopped short in shock.

The light of the rising moon showed a pirogue moored just behind their keelboat. Two men were clambering aboard the boat, while a third worked on tying the second one to shore. The third man was facing them, the moonlight shining full upon him, and Adam recognized him instantly.

"Blazes! It's the Brewster brothers!" Adam hissed,

already backing rapidly away. His head spun with the unlikelihood of it all. How had the brothers found them after all this time? "Hurry, before they see us!"

At that moment, Stephen Brewster glanced up from tying his boat. His lips drew back in a snarl and the sound of his oath carried easily on the cold evening breeze.

"Up there!" he shouted to his brothers. "Devil take me, it's those cussed kids! *After them!*"

Seventeen

Once again, they found themselves running for their lives with the Brewsters in hot pursuit. They had the advantage of a head start, and at first that seemed to be enough to pull ahead of the men.

But then in midstride, Adam felt himself stopped short as the very earth seemed to clutch at his foot and yank it down. He was flung hard to the ground, the breath knocked out of him.

"Adam!" Ellie screamed, stopping and turning back.

"Keep going!" he shouted, yanking at his foot trying to free it. It was trapped in a den of some sort, possibly left by one of those prairie dogs they'd seen so much of over the past weeks.

He finally managed to free his foot. But before he could roll over and stand up, Stephen Brewster had reached him.

"Why you cussed devil!" the man roared, bending down

to grab at him. "I'll pay you back right enough for stealing our boat!"

Adam scrabbled desperately against him, barely keeping Stephen from grabbing his collar or hair. "You deserved it for kidnapping Ellie and stealing my medallion," he retorted breathlessly.

"How dare you, boy!" Stephen drew back his fist, clearly ready to strike him square in the face.

But before it could happen, Adam swung both his legs around as quickly and as hard as he could. They struck Stephen just below the knee, knocking his feet out from under him.

The man cursed at the top of his lungs and windmilled his arms, trying to keep himself upright. But it was no use. Stephen crashed to the ground with a loud thud.

Adam was on his feet instantly. "Run! Run!" he cried. Ellie and Franklin were both watching anxiously from just a few yards ahead. "Hurry, the others will be here soon!"

Indeed, when he glanced back over his shoulder he saw the other two Brewster brothers coming at a dead run. Miles paused to help the still-cursing Stephen to his feet, but Roger kept coming, his broad face an angry mask.

"Nice move, Adam," Franklin panted as the two of them raced along beside each other with Ellie immediately behind.

"Thanks," Adam panted in return. "I learned it from the best."

Knocking down Stephen Brewster had gained them just enough time to pull ahead and disappear into the nearest stand of forest. They were soon huddled in some thick underbrush listening to the shouts as the Brewsters searched vainly for them some distance away.

Still, Adam realized, their luck might have run out. The brothers now had control of their boat and supplies and were unlikely to let either out of their sight until they'd tracked down their quarry. He was still pondering the matter when the sounds of pursuit faded far enough into the distance to allow them to creep out of the underbrush. They quickly found a more secure hiding place behind some trees in the hollow of a bluff in which they felt safe spending the night.

"I'll go try and find water," Franklin offered, scooting away before the others could answer.

Adam let him go, knowing the boy was skilled and

careful enough not to be spotted. "What shall we do now?" he whispered to Ellie. "I suppose this makes it too risky to do as we'd intended and search out that treasure tomorrow."

Ellie nodded. "We'd best put our efforts toward staying out of the Brewsters' grasp and making our way upriver to find Lewis and Clark as soon as possible," she murmured in return. "That is the only way we shall be safe now, with no boat or supplies."

Adam's heart sank at the thought of giving up the idea of the three of them finding the treasure, especially now that they were perhaps so close. But he nodded, knowing she was right.

"We can warn the expedition that they are being followed by the Brewsters for nefarious purposes," he said. That had to be the explanation for the brothers' appearance in this isolated place. After all, hadn't their first encounter with the brothers been back in Philadelphia when they were spying upon Captain Lewis? It seemed they still believed the expedition to be on a treasure hunt and were determined to follow. "Surely the men can then capture the brothers or run them off." He shrugged. "And to thank them for their protection, I suppose we shall have to share our treasure map with them." He sighed heavily at the thought.

"It is the only way," Ellie agreed softly. "Do not worry, Adam. Captain Lewis is said to be an intelligent and honorable man. He will surely give you credit for the discovery of the treasure, and your fair share. Just think how proud Father will be when he hears of it!"

Adam smiled weakly. But in truth, Ellie's words didn't make him feel that much better. "All right, it is decided," he said. "There's no point wasting another night here, since we have no supplies and no boat. The most important thing is catching up with the expedition before they pull ahead once more and we are unable to keep up on foot. We should be able to travel well enough by the light of the moon. As soon as Frank returns, we shall be off."

Ellie was in full agreement. They sat in silence for a while, waiting for the boy to return. Then they waited a bit longer. And then longer still.

"Where can he be?" Adam whispered after he judged at least an hour had passed.

Ellie shook her head. "I'm sure he is all right," she whispered. "He doesn't know we are now in a hurry."

"We should go ahead without him," he muttered, almost

meaning it. "Might teach him a lesson about spiriting off that way."

Ellie shot him a look, her face sympathetic in the dim light. "You do not mean that, Adam." It was a statement rather than a question, and Adam didn't argue with it.

After a while they both dozed off, sleeping in fits and starts, sitting up suddenly with every crack of a branch of whisper of wind. Adam's dreams were filled with gold coins and snarling Brewster faces.

The moon had set and the air smelled of dawn when he was suddenly awakened by a hand on his shoulder. He sat up instantly, fists cocked and ready to fight.

"It is only me," Franklin's familiar voice whispered.

"You!" Adam grabbed him by the arm, squeezing perhaps more tightly than necessary. "Where have you been? You said you were only going to look for water!"

"We were worried about you, Frank," Ellie added, awake now, too.

"I am sorry." Franklin shrugged. "But I have good news. I have seen the expedition."

"What—Lewis and Clark?" Adam was so startled that he forgot to continue his scolding.

229

The boy nodded. "It appears they're settling in for the winter," he said. "I hid and spied on them a while. They're building some kind of fort just upriver near a large village of native people."

"Really?" Ellie looked interested. "Oh, I should like to meet some natives on this trip!"

"You shall have your chance soon enough." Adam stood up and brushed the leaves and dew off his clothes. "Come then, let's get moving. We want to be well away from here before dawn so the brothers cannot track us."

"Wait!" Franklin said. "I thought of something. The winter camp is only a few miles from here. And we've lost the Brewsters for now. How about we try to find that treasure before we go up there? All we got to do is stay ahead of the Brewsters long enough to do it. We can go join the expedition *after* that."

Adam opened his mouth to protest, then hesitated. Franklin had a point. Why not take one last stab at finding the treasure themselves? If the expedition was as close as the boy said and not likely to go anywhere soon, they could seek out their help and protection at any time they needed it. It seemed the best of both worlds indeed.

"Ellie?" he said, turning to his sister. "What do you think?"

He expected her to remind them of all the reasons it would be safer to make their way to the encampment immediately. Instead, she was silent for a moment. Then she smiled first at her brother and then at Franklin.

"We have been living out my greatest desire all this time," she said, patting the pocket where she kept her notebook. "It seems to me it's time to live yours. Let's find that treasure!"

By the time the sun was high, they were a mile or two away, doing their best to follow the rather vague indications on the map. At first they weren't certain what the markings by the X might mean. But when they drew closer to what they thought might be the right area, it began to be clearer.

"See that rocky bit up there by them hills?" Franklin pointed ahead. "P'raps it's the zigzag thing on the map."

"I think you are right," Adam agreed. "That means we should track a bit to the left to aim for that X."

They did so, and soon recognized another of the markings—a faded squiggle that they saw must indicate a

231

certain meandering stream. The final marking was a sort of
Y shape. They could find nothing that resembled it in the
landscape.

"It might have been a large tree that is no longer standing," Ellie guessed. "Still, I think with what we know we can
make a good estimation of where that X should be."

Adam nodded. It was nearly midday by now, and the sun
shone feebly down upon them, trying its best to warm the
chilled earth. "Let's pick a spot and start digging," he said,
grabbing a stout branch from the ground to use as a tool.
"But someone should stand lookout in case the Brewsters
turn up."

Ellie agreed to take the first turn. She found a spot on
a nearby hill and agreed to whistle if she saw anything
suspicious. Meanwhile, Adam and Franklin began to dig.

"What d'you think we'll find?" Franklin asked eagerly,
stabbing at the ground with a large, pointy stone.

Adam grunted. "Don't know. But it's good we're digging
now and not in a week or two. Won't be long before the
ground is frozen solid."

Franklin nodded, and for a few minutes they worked in
silence. As he scooped cool, moist earth out of the hole he

was working on, tossing aside chunks of stone as he went, Adam experienced a vivid moment of unreality as he thought about just what they were doing. Could this really be him, Adam Benjamin Gates of Concord, Massachusetts, kneeling on the cold ground of some uncharted territory digging for treasure beside an immigrant orphan? At that moment, it seemed almost too fantastical to be true, as if the past four or five months had been nothing but some feverish dream. . . .

Then, without warning, Ellie was beside them, out of breath and with a strange look in her eyes. "What is it?" Adam asked her with some alarm. "Did you spy the Brewsters approaching? Or are you here to take a turn digging?"

His sister shook her head. "Not the Brewsters," she gasped out. "Someone else. Look!"

Adam glanced the way she indicated, expecting to see a member of the Lewis and Clark expedition or perhaps some new form of wild beast. Instead, his jaw dropped as he saw three men step into view. They were tall and muscular, with dark eyes and skin and long, curved noses in handsome but exotic faces. They were dressed in animal pelts adorned with dye and feathers, and each wore a headdress atop dark hair that drifted down to broad shoulders.

"Savages!" Franklin breathed in awe.

The men paused, spotting them. They appeared to talk among themselves for a moment, as if deciding what to do. Adam's head spun as he waited to see what would happen. Fleeing or fighting the Brewsters was one thing. But he had no idea what to do in this situation.

After what seemed forever, but was surely only a matter of moments, the natives nodded in their direction. One raised a hand as if in greeting. Then they all turned and moved on, soon disappearing behind the next hill.

"Blazes!" Adam breathed once the natives were out of sight. "Why do you suppose they didn't come over to see who we are and what we're doing here?"

Ellie had finally caught her breath. Her eyes were shining with interest as she stared in the direction the native men had gone.

"They probably thought we were with Lewis and Clark's party," she said. "Frank said the new fort is near a native village, did you not, Frank? So I suppose they've met all the local tribes."

Franklin nodded. "I saw men like that going in and out

by the fort," he reported. "S'pose those three thought we must be with Lewis and them, like Ellie says."

"You're probably right." Adam shifted his digging branch to his other hand. "But let's not question this stroke of luck. Let's keep digging. I'll feel better once the treasure is found and we are safe in that fort away from Brewsters, wild creatures, and warriors alike."

He jammed his digging branch into the loosened dirt of his hole. It hit something hard, and he yelped.

"Must be another rock," he muttered.

Dropping to his knees, he dug into the soil with both hands. His fingertips scraped against something hard and unyielding. He followed it, digging down and trying to gauge its shape and size.

His eyes widened as the "rock" made a square corner. "Hey," he said, scraping at the soil as quickly as he could. "This doesn't feel like a rock. . . ."

Franklin dropped his digging tool and rushed over. "I'll help," he said eagerly.

"What is it?" Ellie asked, crouching down to watch as the two of them dug frantically.

A dull glint broke through the dirt. "It looks like

brass!" Adam exclaimed. Brushing furiously at the remaining covering of soil, he saw an expanse of wood, dark and half rotted with age, stretching out on either side of the newly revealed brass binding. It was some kind of ancient trunk!

Eighteen

It took all three of them to lift the trunk out of its hole and set it on level ground. It was not particularly large—perhaps three feet long and two wide.

"Go ahead," Ellie urged her twin. "Open it."

Adam glanced over at Frank, who was staring wide-eyed at the trunk. "Why don't you take that end and help me? On the count of three . . ."

The trunk creaked open at their first attempt, rust and dirt flaking off the edges of the lid. "Didn't need no key, after all," Frank said.

"Indeed. It doesn't seem to have a lock on it," Ellie said, touching the simple latch.

Meanwhile, Adam was staring into the trunk. At first glance, the value of its contents appeared to fall somewhere between the shells and headdresses he'd feared and the Treasure of the Ancients he'd hoped to find.

And indeed, further examination bore out that theory.

The trunk contained a variety of items. Some two dozen pieces of jewelry, much of it tarnished, most seeming of modest value. A handful of old coins that appeared to be of Spanish extraction. Some clothes, papers, and other items that were well into the process of crumbling away into dust. A few small snuffboxes, spoons, and other ordinary things made of silver or pewter. Loose beads, feathers, and other fairly worthless bits of ephemera.

Ellie reached in and picked up a ring, examining it in the sunlight. "Looks quite old," she commented. "Old enough to come from Roanoke, perhaps."

"Do you think so?" Adam glanced at her. "You believe the lost colonists might have left their homes and carried this trunk *all* the way from the Virginia coast?"

She shrugged. "Nobody has ever discovered what happened to those settlers in over two hundred years," she pointed out. "And these certainly look as if they could be some of their most valuable possessions. They might have struck out across the wilderness for some unknown reason, leaving that medallion and the rest of the trail to guide those coming after them."

"Only those people never got the medallion." Adam

rested both hands on the edge of the trunk, gazing at the items within. Much like solving President Jefferson's clue, finding the treasure seemed to provide more questions than answers. "Instead, it came into our ancestor's possession, then proceeded to float down through the generations until, at a most fortuitous time, it happened to come into my possession." Glancing over at Franklin, who was still staring in awe at the treasure, he dropped a hand onto the boy's shoulder. "Into *our* possession," he amended with a smile.

He felt a rich contentment settle over him. True, it was a bit disappointing that the trail had not led them to wealth beyond imagining. This treasure certainly would not change the Gates family fortunes much—or even, most likely, prevent their neighbors back home in Concord from snickering behind their backs over the family's odd interests.

But there was a certain splendor in knowing that he and his companions had done it. They'd followed a trail through many difficulties to its conclusion. He knew that his father and grandfather, at least, would value that accomplishment just as much, no matter the provenance of the treasure at the end of the quest. He also knew that he would be giving much thought in the coming days to the possible details of the trunk's history and significance. Seeing these old things, touching them—had awakened within him a certain curiosity, a hunger to discover more. But not now. Now it was time once again to be responsible, to find Lewis and Clark and seek safety with them before winter or the Brewsters caught up with them.

"Come," he said, reaching in for the gold coins. "There's no sense in lugging the trunk about. Let's just take the valuable bits in our pockets."

The others nodded. Within minutes, they had all but emptied the trunk. "Now what?" Ellie said, brushing off her hands and standing up. "Shall we try to—"

She broke off in a gasp as a slender figure came flying at them from the nearest copse of cottonwoods. It was a striking native girl with wide-set, intelligent eyes; she appeared to be in her late teens. She was chattering in her own language, gesturing urgently with her hands all the while.

Adam leaped to his feet, startled. "Hey," he blurted out. "Who are you, and what do you want?"

The native girl switched into what sounded like French, still speaking with great urgency. Franklin stared at her blankly, while Ellie wrinkled her brow in concentration.

"My French is not very good," she said. "But I think she wants us to come with her right now?"

"*Oui, oui!*" the native girl cried, now shooting anxious glances toward a forested area across the way. "Come now. You come now!"

She grabbed at Adam's sleeve and began to pull him after her, her dark eyes seeming to plead with him to trust her. Something about her expression made him impulsively decide to do so, though he wasn't sure why.

"Come along," he called over his shoulder to the others. "Let's just do as she says. She appears to mean us no harm."

She led them back to the trees. They were barely hidden behind some rocks and underbrush when the Brewsters burst out of the forest across the way, accompanied by a young native man.

Adam's eyes widened. He glanced first at Ellie, whose face had gone white, and then at the native girl. She had just saved their lives!

Stephen Brewster spotted the large hole and the trunk immediately. He rushed over, swearing loudly as he looked in and found the interior empty of all but a few leftover beads and feathers.

"They got here already!" he said, adding several particularly colorful oaths. "The cussed little scoundrels beat us to it!"

His brothers were equally agitated, stomping about and swearing while their native guide watched impassively. Adam hardly dared to breathe until the brothers finally seemed to give up. They turned and stormed off, the native man casting one curious glance at the trunk and then trailing along after them.

Neither Adam nor his companions stirred for several long moments after that. Finally, when it seemed the Brewsters truly had departed the area, Adam finally stretched and stood.

"Thank you," he said to the native girl, hoping she could understand him. "Er, *merci*," he added, using one of the handful of French words he knew. "You have just saved us. But how and why?"

The woman shook her head, looking nonplussed. "*Je suis* Sacagawea."

"Sacagawea," Ellie repeated carefully. Glancing at the

others, she explained, "She is saying that is her name—Sacagawea."

Ellie introduced herself, Adam, and Frank carefully. Then she listened, her head cocked to one side, as Sacagawea said something in her own language and then in French.

"I am sorry," Ellie said with an exaggerated shrug. "I do not understand."

"You." Sacagawea pointed to Ellie. "Woman? I think no woman on Monsieur Clark, er . . ." Seeming to give up, she again switched to French.

"I cannot understand everything she is saying," Ellie told the others as she listened. "But I think she believes us to be with Lewis and Clark's expedition. She is expressing surprise that she did not see me before, as she believed there to be no women with the party."

She did her best to continue the conversation with their rescuer. However, Ellie's French was not particularly strong, and Sacagawea's English was even worse. Finally, the native girl threw up her hands in frustration.

"Come," she said, gesturing with one finger. "I take to husband."

She led them off across the hilly land. Within half an hour, they were in the spice-and-boiled-meat-scented hut of a burly, lank-haired French-Canadian fur trader by the name of Toussaint Charbonneau. He listened while his young native wife explained in French what had happened.

"I see," he said in heavily accented but passable English. "Quite a confusing situation, eh? But p'raps now we can get to the bottom of things. . . ."

Epilogue

A few months later, Adam peered out the window of a cramped coach, eager for his first glimpse of the familiar Concord church steeple. Ellie leaned over him.

"Can you see it?" she asked.

"Not quite yet." Adam sat back and smiled at his sister. He could hardly believe they were here. It had been a long journey—though not nearly as long as it could have been, thanks to their new friend Sacagawea.

Ellie seemed to be thinking along the same lines. "It is hard to believe we are finally almost home, is it not?" she said.

Adam nodded. Upon learning their true identity and story, Sacagawea had insisted on helping them return home. Toussaint Charbonneau had agreed to help with the arrangements as long as he was given a share of their treasure, which had seemed fair enough to Adam and the others. At first Ellie had wanted to go see Lewis and

Clark—whose camp was not far from Charbonneau's hut—and try again to join their expedition, that was continuing westward in the spring. But Charbonneau had laughed heartily at the very idea, explaining that the men seemed a bit dubious even about his proposal to allow himself to accompany them only as long as Sacagawea could come along. He had had to point out that she would be able to act as translator to the natives they would meet along the way. Finally, recognizing she had no such skill—and the truth that women really weren't part of the expedition—Ellie had given up the idea of accompanying the group. She told Adam and Franklin she was satisfied with the adventure she'd had to that point.

Thus, with the help of a series of native guides and tough, fast horses, the Gates twins and Franklin Poole had raced the looming winter as they sped eastward. They had reached Detroit, a good-sized settlement in the Northwest Territory, just in advance of a howling blizzard, and had spent the rest of the winter there. As soon as the weather had warmed enough to make the land passable, they had departed on the first available conveyance, aiming toward Boston.

And now here they were, only a few miles outside

Concord. It was still chilly, with patches of snow here and there, but Adam could smell spring on the breeze. He couldn't wait to see his family again, his home, even the stable and harness shop. Even so, a part of his mind still lingered far into the reaches of the Western frontier.

He didn't know what had happened to the Brewster brothers. Upon their departure, Charbonneau had winked and assured them he would "do something about those rogues, fear ye not." But Adam had no idea what that meant and had decided that perhaps it was better that way.

The ultimate fate of the Roanoke colonists, if that was truly who had left behind that treasure chest filled with all their worldly treasures, was also still shrouded in uncertainty. However, Sacagawea had been able to clear up at least one additional mystery. When Adam had showed her the map Frank had found, she had pointed instantly to the cryptic marking drawn over the mountain at the bottom corner—the same marking that was on the face of the medallion. With her husband translating, she had explained that the mark indicated a certain mountain range that lay about a week's journey to the south and was known by the Lakota Sioux as the Six Grandfathers.

"That makes sense," Adam had said as he'd stared at the marking—six slashes through a humanlike figure. "I wonder why it's on the map, though?"

None of them had found any definitive answers to that, though they speculated that the marking had been added later due to its darker appearance. "P'raps they was going there next, after they dropped off their things where we found 'em," Frank had suggested. Then he'd shrugged. "Seems they never come back for 'em, though. Odd."

Indeed, almost everything about the medallion quest still seemed rather odd. But somehow that made it all the more interesting even in retrospect.

Now, pulling his gaze away from the Massachusetts scenery in an attempt to quell his impatience, Adam reached into his clothes and pulled out that first drawing Franklin had made after spotting that marking outside of Pittsburgh. The paper was tattered and stained by now, the markings faded by being soaked in the river and exposed to the sun. Still, Adam was glad that he had it. It would be a wonderful reminder of his adventure.

And at least we've solved some part of that old family puzzle, he thought, gazing down upon the familiar slashes and swirls of the lost medallion's markings. *It's nice to have that to think about. Not to mention the treasure itself. It may not be the Treasure of the Ancients, but it should help soothe Mother's anger with us for leaving for so long.*

He glanced over at Ellie, who was now staring out the opposite window. "It's a bit strange, isn't it?" she mused, turning as she felt his eyes upon her. "Coming home, that is." She sighed, then smiled. "This certainly has been the adventure of a lifetime!"

Adam chuckled. "Indeed." He winked. "In any case, I am certain that Private McNeal shall fill you in on all he has seen once he returns from the expedition—unless he manages to figure out a way to deliver letters to you before then, that is. Wasn't that he that we spotted from a distance on our way out from Sacagawea's home? I saw you looking, sister dear. It is too bad we did not have time to stop and say hello."

Ellie blushed. "Never you mind about that," she said tartly. "Look, there is the oak that was struck by lightning! We are almost there."

Adam glanced out at the landmark they were passing, but his mind wasn't on trees or lightning. The mention of letters had reminded him once more of President Jefferson's coded message. It seemed it had had nothing to do with the medallion, after all. What then could it mean? Could it have been pointing toward an entirely different quest—perhaps even the Treasure of the Ancients as the Brewsters had thought?

I wish I'd remembered to give it to Charbonneau to pass along to Captain Lewis, he thought, touching his jacket pocket where the letter lay. *In all the rush of trying to race the winter snows, it did not cross my mind until too late.*

But he shrugged off the worry. Perhaps once Lewis returned from his epic journey, Adam would seek him out in Washington and present the letter himself, explaining all that had happened to lead him to possess it. Perhaps when he did, he would even add a side trip to Maryland to pay a visit to Mr. Carroll of Carrollton. . . .

He smiled, realizing the folly in planning new journeys when he had not yet quite made it home from this one. He supposed that meant the old family itch for adventure and treasure had been well and truly awakened at last. Never again would he be content with spending his life flowing lazily along like the river.

Perhaps one day I shall be the one to find the real Treasure of the

Ancients, wherever it may be, he mused. He glanced once more at his sister, who had returned her gaze to the scenery. *Perhaps one day Ellie will have her chance to make it all the way to the western sea as Lewis and Clark are attempting to do.*

Then his gaze slid across the coach to a small, slightly grubby figure huddled between a couple of large packages that the driver had shoved inside to fill out the coach. The boy was playing idly with a couple of the Spanish galleons they'd found in the trunk.

But for the moment, I suppose there is only one challenge we should have at the forefront of our minds, Adam thought, smiling as Franklin looked up and met his eye. *And that's how to explain to the family that we've returned with more than mere treasure—we've also brought home an extra brother!*

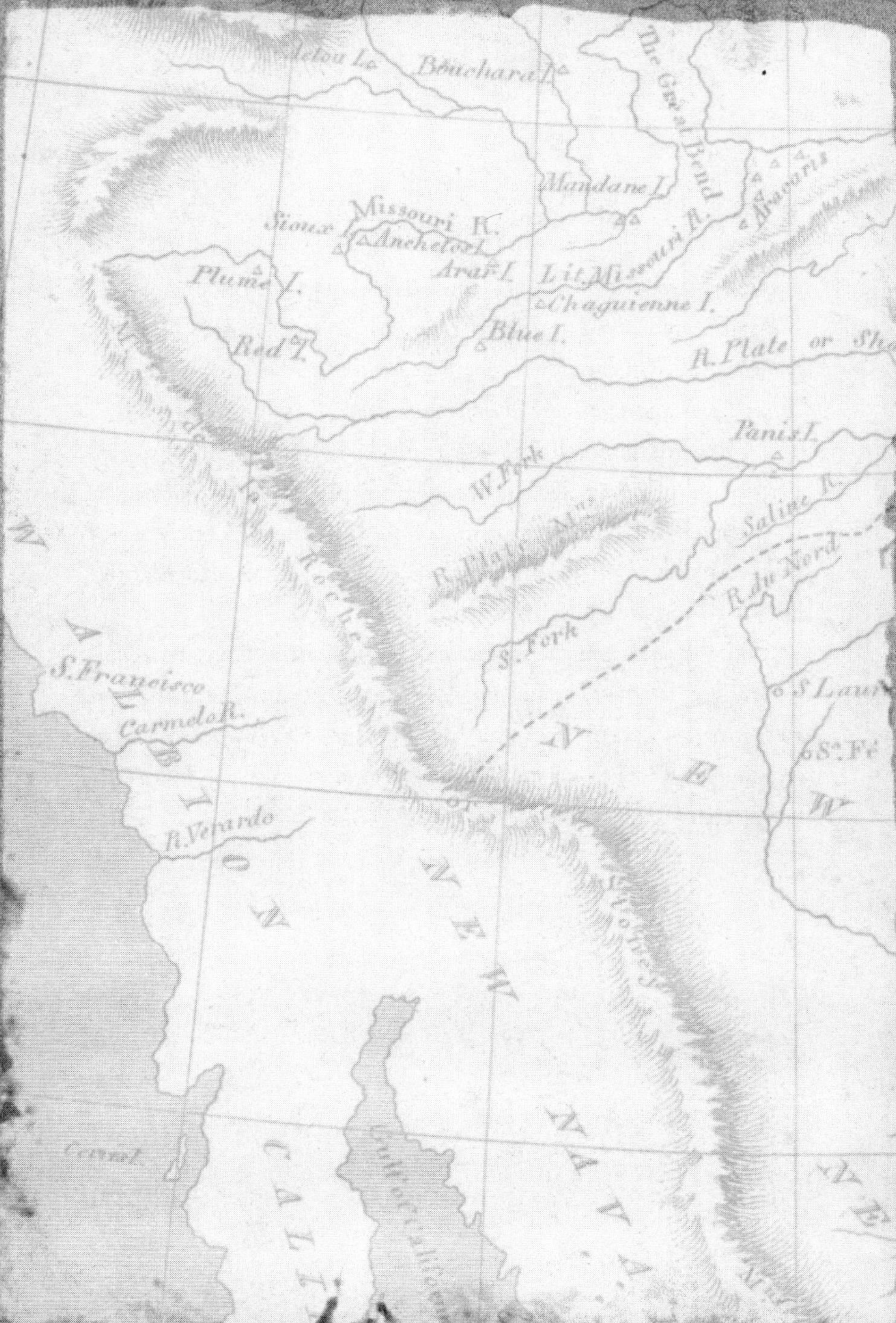
Bouchard L.
Mandane L.
The Great Bend
Missouri R.
Sioux L.
Anchetoe L.
Plume L.
Arar L.
Lit. Missouri R.
Chaguienne L.
Blue L.
Red L.
R. Plate or
Panis L.
W. Fork
Saline R.
R. du Nord
S. Fork
S. Francisco
Carmelo R.
R. Verardo
Sa. Fé

Bear L.

SAES

Lake R REYNARDS

Mississippi R.

Mahas

Falls of S. Antony

L. Pepin

Horleton's

Carver R.

S. Peter R.

Wood R.

Fox R.

Green R.

Bark R.

Lake Michigan

Tinton L.

Yellow R.

Lead

Iowa R.

Tintons

Wolf L.

SIOUX

R. de Moines

Ouisconsin R.

Illinois R.

Otos L.

Meadow R.

Ayoas L.

Panis L.

R. à Tabiane

ari L.

Cansas

Oer R.

Cansas R.

Great P.

Extenière

St. Charles

Kahokia

Missouri R.

Missouri

Devil

S. Louis

Ka ska sia

Salt Rock

R. Osages

S. Genevieve

Padoucash

Osages L.

MINE

Salt

R. Fichou

Potatoe R.

N. Madrid

R T H

Mentons L.

R. S. Francis

Paniasa L.

White R.

Arkansas R.

ME XI

Cadodaquis

Panimde

Akansa

Red R.

Yazou R.

Adaye

Mexicas R.

Natchitoch

Natchez

Trinity

W. FL.

CENIS

Colorado

Mississippi R.

S. Paul

R. del Nord

G U L F

O

Post Script

Like the films *National Treasure and National Treasure: Book of Secrets* that inspired it, this is a fictional story grounded in real facts and history. Adam Benjamin Gates, his sister, Ellie, and the rest of their family, plus Franklin Poole, the Brewster brothers, and some of the other characters, are invented. But many others who appear in the story were real people who lived at that time, and many of the events that Adam witnesses, hears about, or discusses actually did take place.

President Thomas Jefferson really did send Meriwether Lewis and William Clark off on their famous expedition, which carried them from their camp near St. Louis all the way to the West Coast. Lewis really did have a big, black dog who was known as Seaman; he acquired the dog while in Pittsburgh overseeing the construction of the large keelboat used on the journey. Before that, Lewis spent part of the spring of 1803 in Philadelphia learning from the leading scientists of the time, who included not only Dr. Benjamin Rush, but also botanist Benjamin Smith Barton and astronomer Caspar Wistar, whose names are still well known in Philadelphia to this day.

And, of course, the Louisiana Purchase was a real event that approximately doubled the size of the nation, involving the acquisition of more than 800,000 square miles of territory at a total cost of just over $23 million—that works out to about four cents per acre! The territory involved included what later became the entire states of Arkansas, Iowa, Kansas, Missouri, Nebraska, and Oklahoma; most of Colorado, Louisiana, Minnesota, Montana, North and South Dakota, and Wyoming; and parts of New Mexico and Texas.

Sacagawea was real as well and the only female member of the expedition. She joined during the winter the group spent in North Dakota. Her French-Canadian husband, Toussaint Charbonneau, was also a real person, though in reality he did not speak much, if any, English—a detail that has been altered for the sake of this story.

The mountain known as the Six Grandfathers, referenced in the story, is a real spot; located in South Dakota, it is now better known by its modern name: Mount Rushmore.

Several other real figures are mentioned throughout the story as well, including Napoleon, Private Hugh McNeal, and Charles Carroll of Carrollton, Maryland.

Chien

delou I. Bouchara I.

The Great Bend

Mandane I.

Ricaris

Sioux I. Missouri R.

Anchetok I.

Arak I. Lit. Missouri R.

Plume I.

Chaguienne I.

Red T. Blue I.

R. Plate or Sh...

Panis I.

W. Fork

R. Platte Mts.

Saline R.

R. du Nord

S. Fork

S. Lau...

S.ta Fé

S. Francisco

Carmelo R.

Roche

R. Verardo

N E W

Cervel.

C A L I

Gulf of California

N A V A

W   A   L   B   I   O   N

N   E

W

S A E S

Lake R E Y N A R D S

Bear I.

Mississippi R.

Mahas

Falls of S. Antony

L. Pepin

Fox R.

Horicton

Carver R.

S. Peter R.

Wood R.

Green R.

Bark R.

Tinton L.

Yellow R.

Tintons

Lead

Iowa R.

Wolf I.

S I O U X

R. de Moines

Otos I.

Ayoas I.

Cansus

R. à Tabiane

Cansas R.

Extensive

Meadow

Great R.

Ox R.

Illinois R.

Missouri R.

Ahasou Devil R.

S. Charles

S. Louis

Kahokia

Salt Rock

R. Osage

S. Genevéve

Kaskaski

Padoucas R.

Osages I.

Salt

N O R T H

R. Fichou

Potatoe L.

MINE

N. Madrid

R. S. Francis

Mentons Ls.

White R.

Paniara I.

Arkansas R.

Cadodaquis

Panimaha
Akansa

M E X I C O

Red R.

Adayes

Natchez

Mexican R.

W. FL

S. Paul

Trinity R.

Natchitoches

Yazoo R.

C E N I S O

Mississippi R.

R. del Norte

Colorado

G U L F   O F

Gates Family Tree

Samuel Thomas Gates
[1594-1661]
London, England

Alice Gates
[1571-1630]
London, England

Benjamin Gates
[1568-1621]
London, England

Elizabeth Gates/Martin
[1595-1661]
London, England

John Gates
[1618-1654]
Jamestown, Virginia Colony

Victoria Gates/Wall
[1620-1650]
Charles City, Virginia Colony

Edward James Gates
[1635-1685]
Jamestown, Virginia Colony

Mary Gates/Dunleavy
[1637-1675]
Providence, Rhode Island Colony

Benjamin Gates
[1615-1660]
Jamestown, Virginia Colony

Elizabeth Gates/White
[1620-1641]
Glasgow, Scotland

Martha Gates
[1657-1662]
Jamestown, Virginia Colony

John Patrick Gates
[1640-1691]
Jamestown, Virginia Colony

Alice Gates/Porter
[1639-1697]
Peabody, Massachusetts Colony

Constance Gates/White
[1722-1760] m2
Concord, Massachusetts Colony

William Gates
[~1591-1645]
London, England

Mary Gates/Wallis
[1593-1642]
London, England

Alice Gates
[1617-1642]
Jamestown, Virginia Colony

George Gates
[1615-1679]
Jamestown, Virginia Colony

Maureen Gates/Burns
[1620-1679]
Wicklow, Ireland

Seamus Gates
[1641-1647]
Jamestown, Virginia Colony

Gates Generation
records missing

Thomas Samuel Gates
[1722-1805]
Concord, Massachusetts Colony

Charlotte Gates/Sweeney
[1726-1753] m1
Lexington, Virginia Colony

Mary Gates
[~1748-1806]
Concord, Massachusetts Colony

Elizabeth Gates
[1750-1816]
Concord, Massachusetts Colony

Sarah Gates
[1752-1781]
Concord, Massachusetts Colony

Alice Gates
[~1755-1821]
Concord, Massachusetts Colony

John Raleigh Gates
[1757-1830]
Concord, Massachusetts Colony

Mercy Gates
[1760-1786]
Concord, Massachusetts Colony

Humility Gates
[1760-1809]
Concord, Massachusetts Colony

May Gates/Dunrick
[1757-1824]
Philadelphia, Pennsylvania Colony

George Gates
[1785-1847]
Concord, Massachusetts Colony

Adam Benjamin Gates
[1786-1851]
Concord, Massachusetts Colony

Eleanor (Ellie) Gates
[1786-1855]
Concord, Massachusetts Colony

Timothy Gates
[1788-1832]
Concord, Massachusetts Colony

Hallowell Gates
[1790-1844]
Concord, Massachusetts Colony

Olive R.

delou L.   Bouchara I.   The Great Bend

Mandane I.   Aragaris

Missouri R.   Lit. Missouri R.

Sioux L.   Anchetool

Plume I.   Arar I.   Lit. Missouri

Chaguienne I.

Red T.   Blue I.   R. Plate or Sho

Panis I.

W. Fork   Saline R.

R. Platte Mts   R. du Nord

Roche

S. Fork

S. Francisco   N   E

Carmel R.   S. Laui

S.ta Fé

W

R. Verardo

S. Torres

CALIFO

Golfo California

NEW   NAVA

DON'T MISS THE NEXT VOLUME...

WESTWARD BOUND
❧ *A* GATES *Family Mystery* ❧

James Munroe Gates has heard the same story all his life. According to family legend, a treasure lies hidden with someone, or something, named Charlotte. For years, his father and eldest brother have sought the elusive fortune, looking for clues that will bring them to the end of their quest. But James wants a more immediate treasure.

When he discovers letters from his aunt that speak of fortune in the West, James sees his chance. But almost immediately, he runs into problems—in the form of a runaway aristocrat and a conspiracy-focused friend named Seamus. Soon, the trio find themselves bound together in a journey that will lead them to the most unlikely of treasures.

And beginning Fall 2008 . . .

PIRATES of the CARIBBEAN
LEGENDS OF THE BRETHREN COURT

The Caribbean
Rob Kidd

Based on the earlier adventures of characters created
for the theatrical motion picture,
"Pirates of the Caribbean: The Curse of the Black Pearl"
Screen Story by Ted Elliott & Terry Rossio and
Stuart Beattie and Jay Wolpert,
Screenplay by Ted Elliott & Terry Rossio,
And characters created for the theatrical motion pictures
"Pirates of the Caribbean: Dead Man's Chest" and
"Pirates of the Caribbean: At World's End"
written by Ted Elliott & Terry Rossio

CHAPTER ONE

"Jack!"

The sun shone merrily on the sparkling blue sea, and on the crisp black sails and gleaming scrubbed decks of the *Black Pearl*. Up at the prow of the ship, a dashing pirate stood proudly, arms akimbo and legs braced against the rolling waves, his dark hair flying in the wind. He turned his head slightly and grinned, letting the sunlight sparkle grandly off his gold tooth.

"JACK!" the voice behind him called again, exasperated.

Jack Sparrow still did not respond. He tried a different way of tilting his head, setting his hat at a jaunty new angle.

The barrel of a pistol poked him forcefully in the ribs.

"I don't know what you're playing at," his first mate snarled from the other end of the pistol, "but I *know* you can hear me, Jack."

"Oh, sorry," Jack said, spinning around and giving a little wave of his hand. "I presumed you must be addressing some *other* Jack, one who was not captain of the finest ship ever to sail the Seven Seas—since *surely* if you were addressing *me*, you would have said 'Captain Jack,' isn't that right?"

His first mate heaved a deep, irritated sigh, his scraggly red beard quivering. "My apologies, *Captain* Jack."

"That's much better," Jack said, tapping him lightly on the head. "When we get our new crew in Tortuga, they'll be looking to you for how to behave, savvy?" He sauntered back toward center deck, then turned, squinting, as a thought struck him. "Oh, and really? Ostrich feathers, Barbossa? Don't you think that's a little much?"

Barbossa narrowed his eyes as Captain Jack Sparrow sallied off along the deck. He self-consciously touched his new hat, resplendent with enormous ostrich feathers. "We're a-coming up on Tortuga now, *sir*," he called.

"Excellent," Jack called back. "Let's see if we can find some *real* pirates there."

The few remaining crew members glared at him.

"I mean, in addition to you fine . . . swarthy . . . er, burly ruffians," Jack added.

It was surprising how fickle pirates could be. One tiny misadventure—one mislabeled treasure map, one chest of mold instead of gold—and they scattered to the winds, grumbling and muttering and throwing dark glances back at their captain. As if it were his fault! So what if he was the one who'd bought the map? Any other pirate captain would have done the same at that ridiculously low price.

Well, no matter. If there was one thing that was easy to find in the Caribbean, it was a fresh supply of pirates. With his loyal first mate, Barbossa, at his side, Jack would sweep into Tortuga, and no doubt the best pirates would fall all over themselves to join him.

They only had to take one look at his magnificent ship to see the advantages of being part of Jack's crew. The *Black Pearl*! Fastest ship in the Caribbean! This was a far cry from his first command, the lowly *Barnacle*. Pirates dreamed all their lives of having a ship like the *Pearl*, and now it was his: risen from the depths of Davy Jones's Locker like the Kraken from the deep.

And all he had to do to get it was barter away his soul. Jack straightened his hat, brushing away the uneasiness that came with that thought. He didn't have to worry about his bargain for another thirteen years. He'd find a way to deal with it by then. For now, he had thirteen years of freedom to look forward to—thirteen years of freedom with his loyal crew and his splendid ship.

First he just had to find that loyal crew.

In this first volume, Jack assembles a new crew that includes his first mate, Hector Barbossa, the brooding

Billy Turner, and a certain sailor named Jean that Jack's known since they were both kids. Also on board are a host of new and daring cohorts joining Jack in his quest for absolute freedom—the royal pirate Caroline and her partner-in-crime Diego; the truly fearsome (you'll need to read it to see why) Catastrophe Shane; Jean's cousin, Marcella; and Tia Dalma's mysterious servant, Alex. But it doesn't take the crew long to find trouble—in the form of Villanueva, the Pirate Lord of the Adriatic Sea.

This series, in six volumes, will see Jack and his new crew sail the Seven Seas and encounter the Pirate Lords who control them. Get ready for a trip around the world, traveling the only way to go—aboard the legendary *Black Pearl*!